BODIES OF WATER

£2-50

Michelle Cliff was born in Jamaica,
and grew up there, and in New York.
She was educated in the USA and
later at the University of London,
and now lives in California.
Internationally known through her
essays, articles and lectures, she has
received exceptional critical acclaim
for her previous works, which
include *No Telephone To Heaven*.
Bodies of Water is her sixth book.

Also by Michelle Cliff

*No Telephone to Heaven
The Land of Look Behind
Abeng
Claiming an Identity They Taught Me to Despise
The Winner Names the Age (ed.)

Available in Minerva

BODIES OF WATER

stories by

MICHELLE CLIFF

Minerva

A Minerva Paperback
BODIES OF WATER

First published in Great Britain 1990
by Methuen London
This Minerva edition published 1991
by Mandarin Paperbacks
Michelin House, 81 Fulham Road, London SW3 6RB

Minerva is an imprint of the Octopus Publishing Group,
a division of Reed International Books Limited

'Columba' first appeared in *The American Voice*.
'Election Day 1984' first appeared in the
Voice Literary Supplement.

Extract from 'Chemin de Fer' by Elizabeth Bishop
taken from *The Complete Poems 1927–1979*
and reprinted by permission
of Farrer, Straus and Giroux.

A CIP catalogue record for this title
is available from the British Library
ISBN 0 7493 9109 X

Printed and bound in Great Britain
by Cox and Wyman Ltd, Reading, Berks

In memory of my Aunt Irene,
and for my grandmother, Nones

'Love should be put into action!'
                  screamed the old hermit.
Across the pond an echo
                  tried and tried to confirm it.

Elizabeth Bishop, *Chemin de Fer*

CONTENTS

PART ONE

Columba

When I was twelve my parents left me in the hands of a hypochondriacal aunt and her Cuban lover, a ham radio operator. Her lover, that is, until she claimed their bed as her own. She was properly a family friend, who met my grandmother when they danced the Black Bottom at the Glass Bucket. Jamaica in the twenties was wild.

This woman, whose name was Charlotte, was large and pink and given to wearing pink satin nighties – flimsy relics, pale from age. Almost all was pink in that room, so it seemed; so it seems now, at this distance. The lace trim around the necks of the nighties was not pink; it was yellowed and frazzled, practically absent. Thin wisps of thread which had once formed flowers, birds, a spider's web. Years of washing in hard water with brown soap had made the nighties loose, droop, so that Charlotte's huge breasts slid outside, suddenly, sideways, pink falling on pink like ladylike camouflage, but for her livid nipples. No one could love those breasts, I think.

Her hair stuck flat against her head, bobbed and straightened, girlish bangs as if painted on her forehead. Once she had resembled Louise Brooks. No longer. New moons arced each black eye.

Charlotte was also given to drinking vast amounts of water from the crystal carafes standing on her low bedside table, next to her *Information Please Almanac* – she had a fetish for detail but no taste for reading – linen hankies scented with bay rum, and a bowl of soursweet tamarind balls. As she drank, so did she piss, ringing changes on the walls of chamber pots lined under the bed, all through the day and night. Her room, her pink expanse, smelled of urine

13

and bay rum and the wet sugar which bound the tamarind balls. Ancestral scents.

I was to call her Aunt Charlotte and to mind her, for she was officially *in loco parentis*.

The Cuban, Juan Antonio Corona y Mestee, slept on a safari cot next to his ham radio, rum bottle, stacks of *Punch*, *Country Life*, and something called *Gent*. His room was a screened-in porch at the side of the verandah. Sitting there with him in the evening, listening to the calls of the radio, I could almost imagine myself away from that place, in the bush awaiting capture, or rescue, until the sharp PING! of Charlotte's water cut across even my imaginings and the scratch of faraway voices.

One night a young man vaulted the rail of a cruise ship off Tobago and we picked up the distress call. A sustained SPLASH! followed Charlotte's PING! and the young man slipped under the waves.

I have never been able to forget him, and capture him in a snap of that room, as though he floated through it, me. I wonder still, why that particular instant? That warm evening, the Southern Cross in clear view? The choice of a sea-change?

His mother told the captain they had been playing bridge with another couple when her son excused himself. We heard all this on the radio, as the captain reported in full. Henry Fonda sprang to my movie-saturated mind, in *The Lady Eve*, with Barbara Stanwyck. But that was blackjack, not bridge, and a screwball comedy besides.

Perhaps the young man had tired of the coupling. Perhaps he needed a secret sharer.

The Cuban was a tall handsome man with blue-black hair and a costume of unvarying khaki. He seemed content to stay with Charlotte, use the whores in Raetown from time to time, listen to his radio, sip his rum, leaf through his magazines. Sitting on the side of the safari cot in his khaki, engaged in his pastimes, he seemed like a displaced white hunter (except he wasn't white, a fact no amount of relaxers or wide-brimmed hats could mask) or a mercenary recuperating from battle fatigue, awaiting further orders.

Perhaps he did not stir for practical reasons. This was 1960; he could not return to Cuba in all his hyphenated splendor, and had no marketable skills for the British Crown Colony in which he found himself. I got along with him, knowing we were both there on sufferance, unrelated dependants. Me, because Charlotte owed my grandmother something, he, for whatever reason he or she might have.

One of Juan Antonio's duties was to drop me at school. Each morning he pressed a half-crown into my hand, always telling me to treat my friends. I appreciated his largesse, knowing the money came from his allowance. It was a generous act and he asked no repayment but one small thing: I was to tell anyone who asked that he was my father. As I remember, no one ever did. Later, he suggested that I say 'Goodbye, Papá' – with the accent on the last syllable – when I left the car each morning. I hesitated, curious. He said, 'Never mind,' and the subject was not brought up again.

I broke the chain of generosity and kept his money for myself, not willing to share it with girls who took every chance to ridicule my American accent and call me 'salt'.

I used the money to escape them, escape school. Sitting in the movies, watching them over and over until it was time to catch the bus back.

Charlotte was a woman of property. Her small house was a cliché of colonialism, graced with calendars advertising the coronation of ER II, the marriage of Princess Margaret Rose, the visit of Alice, Princess Royal. Bamboo and wicker furniture was sparsely scattered across dark mahogany floors – settee there, end table here – giving the place the air of a hotel lobby, the sort of hotel carved from the shell of a great house, before Hilton and Sheraton made landfall. Tortoise-shell lampshades. Ashtrays made from coconut husks. Starched linen runners sporting the embroideries of craftswomen.

The house sat on top of a hill in Kingston, surrounded by an unkempt estate – so unkempt as to be arrogant, for this was the wealthiest part of the city, and the largest single tract of land. So large that a dead quiet enveloped the place in the evening, and we were cut off, sound and light absorbed by the space and the dark and the trees, abandoned and wild, entangled by vines and choked by underbrush, escaped, each reaching to survive.

At the foot of the hill was a cement gully which bordered the property – an empty moat but for the detritus of trespassers. Stray dogs roamed amid Red Stripe beer bottles, crushed cigarette packets, bully-beef tins.

Trespassers, real and imagined, were Charlotte's passion. In the evening, after dinner, bed-jacket draped across her shoulders against the soft trade winds, which she said were laden with typhoid, she roused herself to the verandah and took aim. She fired and fired and fired. Then she excused herself. 'That will hold them for another night.' She was at once terrified of invasion and confident she could stay it. Her gunplay was ritual against it.

There was, of course, someone responsible for cleaning the house, feeding the animals, filling the carafes and emptying the chamber pots, cooking the meals and doing the laundry. These tasks fell to Columba, a fourteen-year-old from St Ann, where Charlotte had bartered him from his mother; a case of condensed milk, two dozen tins of sardines, five pounds of flour, several bottles of cooking oil, permission to squat on Charlotte's cane-piece – fair exchange. His mother set up housekeeping with his brothers and sisters, and Columba was transported in the back of Charlotte's black Austin to Kingston. A more magnanimous, at least practical, landowner would have had a staff of two, even three, but Charlotte swore against being taken advantage of, as she termed it, so all was done by Columba, learning to expand his skills under her teaching, instructions shouted from the bed.

He had been named not for our discoverer, but for the saint buried on Iona, discoverer of the monster in the loch. A Father Pierre, come to St Ann from French Guiana, had taught Columba's mother, Winsome, to write her name, read a ballot, and know God. He said he had been assistant to the confessor on Devil's Island, and when the place was finally shut down in 1951 he was cast adrift, floating around the islands seeking a berth.

His word was good enough for the people gathered in his seaside chapel of open sides and thatched roof, used during the week to shelter a woman smashing limestone for the road, sorting trilobite from rock. On Sunday morning people sang, faces misted by spray, air heavy with the scent of sea grapes, the fat purple bunches bowing, swinging, brushing the glass sand, bruised. Bruises releasing more scent, entering the throats of a congregation fighting the smash of the sea. On Sunday morning Father Pierre talked to them of God, dredging his memory for every tale he had been told.

This was good enough for these people. They probably couldn't tell a confessor from a convict – which is what Father Pierre was – working off his crime against nature by boiling the life out of yam and taro and salted beef for the wardens, his keepers.

Even after the *Gleaner* had broadcast the real story, the congregation stood fast: he was white; he knew God – they reasoned. Poor devils.

Father Pierre held Columba's hand at the boy's baptism. He was ten years old then and had been called 'Junior' all his life. Why honor an un-named sire? Father Pierre spoke to Winsome. 'Children,' the priest intoned, 'the children become their names.' He spoke in an English as broken as hers.

17

What Father Pierre failed to reckon with was the unfamiliar nature of the boy's new name; Columba was 'Collie' to some, 'Like one damn dawg,' his mother said. 'Chuh, man. Hignorant smaddy cyaan accept not'ing new.' Collie soon turned Lassie and he was shamed.

To Charlotte he became 'Colin', because she insisted on Anglicization. It was for his own good, she added for emphasis, and so he would recognize her kindness. His name-as-is was foolish and feminine and had been given him by a *pedophile*, for heaven's sake.

Charlotte's shouts reached Columba in the kitchen. He was attempting to put together a gooseberry fool for the mistress's elevenses. The word *pedophile* smacked the stucco of the corridor between them, each syllable distinct, perversion bouncing furiously off the walls. I had heard – who hadn't? – but the word was beyond me. I was taking Latin, not Greek.

I softly asked Juan Antonio and he, in equally hushed tones, said, 'Mariposa . . . butterfly.'

Charlotte wasn't through. 'Fancy naming a boy after a bird. A black boy after a white bird. And still people attend that man . . . Well, they will get what they deserve,' she promised. 'You are lucky I saved you from that.' She spoke with such conviction.

I was forbidden to speak with Columba except on matters of household business, encouraged by Charlotte to complain when the pleat of my school tunic was not sharp enough. I felt only awkward that a boy two years older than myself was responsible for my laundry, for feeding me, for making my bed. I was, after all, an American now, only here temporarily. I did not keep the commandment.

I sought him out in secret. When Juan Antonio went downtown and while Charlotte dozed, the coast was clear. We sat behind the house under an ancient guava, concealed by a screen of bougainvillea. There we talked. Compared lives. Exchanged histories. We kept each other company, and our need for company made our conversations almost natural. The alternative was a dreadful loneliness; silence, but for the noises of the two adults. Strangers.

His questions about America were endless. What was New York like? Had I been to Hollywood? He wanted to know every detail about Duke Ellington, Marilyn Monroe, Stagger Lee, Jackie Wilson, Ava Gardner, Billy the Kid, Dinah Washington, Tony Curtis, Spartacus, John Wayne. Everyone, every name he knew from the cinema, where he slipped on his evening off; every voice, ballad, beat, he heard over Rediffusion, tuned low in the kitchen.

Did I know any of these people? Could you see them on the street? Then, startling me: what was life like for a black man in America? An ordinary black man, not a star?

I had no idea – not really. I had been raised in a community in New Jersey until this interruption, surrounded by people who had made their own world and 'did not business' with that sort of thing. Bourgeois separatists. I told Columba I did not know and we went back to the stars and legends.

A Tuesday during rainy season: Charlotte, swathed in a plaid lap-robe lifted from the *Queen Mary*, is being driven by Juan Antonio to an ice factory she owns in Old Harbour. There is a problem with the overseer; Charlotte is summoned. You would think she was being transported a thousand miles up the Amazon into headhunter territory, so elaborate are the preparations.

She and Juan Antonio drop me at school. There is no half-crown this morning. I get sixpence and wave them off. I wait for the Austin to turn the corner at St Cecilia's Way, then I cut to Lady Musgrave Road to catch the bus back.

When I return, I change and meet Columba out back. He has promised to show me something. The rain drips from the deep green of the escaped bush which surrounds us. We set out on a path invisible but to him, our bare feet sliding on slick fallen leaves. A stand of mahoe is in front of us. We pass through the trees and come into a clearing.

In the clearing is a surprise: a wreck of a car, thirties Rover. Gut-sprung, tired and forlorn, it slumps in the high grass. Lizards scramble through the vines which wrap around rusted chrome and across black hood and boot. We walk closer. I look into the wreck.

The leather seats are split and a white fluff erupts here and there. A blue gyroscope set into the dash slowly rotates. A pennant of the Kingston Yacht Club dangles miserably from the rearview.

This is not all. The car is alive. Throughout, roaming the seats, perched on the running board, spackling the crystal face of the clock, are doves. White. Speckled. Rock. Mourning. Wreck turned dovecote is filled with their sweet coos.

'Where did you find them?'

Columba is pleased, proud too, I think. 'Nuh find dem nestin' all over de place? I mek dem a home, give dem name. Dat one dere nuh Stagger Lee?' He points to a mottled pigeon hanging from a visor. 'Him is rascal fe true.'

Ava Gardner's feet click across the roof where Spartacus is hot in her pursuit.

Columba and I sit among the birds for hours.

I thank him for showing them to me, promising on my honor not to tell.

That evening I am seated across from Charlotte and next to Juan Antonio in the dining room. The ceiling fan stirs the air, which is heavy with the day's moisture.

Columba has prepared terrapin and is serving us one by one. His head is bowed so our eyes cannot meet, as they never do in such domestic moments. We – he and I – split our lives in this house as best we can. No one watching this scene would imagine our meeting that afternoon, the wild birds, talk of flight.

The turtle is sweet. A turtling man traded it for ice that

morning in Old Harbour. The curved shell sits on a counter in the kitchen. Golden. Delicate. Representing our island. Representing the world.

I did not tell them about the doves.

They found out easily, stupidly.

Charlotte's car had developed a knock in the engine. She noticed it on the journey to the ice factory, and questioned me about it each evening after that. Had I heard it on the way to school that morning? How could she visit her other properties without proper transport? Something must be done.

Juan Antonio suggested he take the Austin to the Texaco station at Matilda's Corner. Charlotte would have none of it. She asked little from Juan Antonio, the least he could do was maintain her automobile. What did she suggest? he asked. How could he get parts to repair the Austin; should he fashion them from bamboo?

She announced her solution: Juan Antonio was to take a machete and chop his way through to the Rover. The car had served her well, she said, surely it could be of use now. He resisted, reminding her that the Rover was thirty years old, probably rusted beyond recognition, and not of any conceivable use. It did not matter.

The next morning Juan Antonio set off to chop his way through the bush, dripping along the path, monkey wrench in his left hand, machete in his right. Columba was in the kitchen, head down, wrapped in the heat of burning coals as he fired irons to draw across khaki and satin.

The car, of course, was useless as a donor, but Juan Antonio's mission was not a total loss. He was relieved to tell Charlotte about the doves. Why, there must be a hundred. All kinds.

Charlotte was beside herself. Her property was the soul of bounty. Her trees bore heavily. Her chickens laid through hurricanes. Edible creatures abounded!

Neither recognized that these birds were not for killing.

They did not recognize the pennant of the Kingston Yacht Club as the colors of this precious colony within a colony.

Columba was given his orders. Wring the necks of the birds. Pluck them and dress them and wrap them tightly for freezing. Leave out three for that evening's supper.

He did as he was told.

Recklessly I walked into the bush. No notice was taken.

I found him sitting in the front seat of the dovecote. A wooden box was beside him, half-filled with dead birds. The live ones did not scatter, did not flee. They sat and paced and cooed, as Columba performed his dreadful task.

'Sorry, man, you hear?' he said softly as he wrung the neck of the next one. He was weeping heavily. Heaving his shoulders with the effort of execution and grief.

I sat beside him in silence, my arm around his waist. This was not done.

The Ferry

The cars on the ferry below decks were kept from the waters of the harbor by a slender gate. Once in a while a car might slip its emergency brake and slide forward. Were it a car at the front of the line, the gate would break its momentum, giving slightly, returning the force it received like a slingshot.

The boy's mother was dating a man who drove a '59 Chevy with dual controls; freaky thing. The man, whose name was Jimmy, borrowed the boy's new sports coat at his mother's request so that she and Jimmy could go to church on Sunday and make a good impression.

The boy, Vincent, did not accompany them. He had given up on church shortly after his father died. Not that he had been particularly close to his father and was left angry at God. Not that he suffered any dramatic loss of faith. His father's death was as good an excuse as any to remove himself from the tedium of the hour of worship, the drone of a minister, the heads spinning to see who was coming down the aisle with whom, what they were wearing, where they would sit – dying for something to talk about.

He knew the sight of his mother and Jimmy would set them calculating the span of widowhood, approving or disapproving, as if their opinions mattered.

The only thing that had kept him going as long as he had was not his mother's wishes (as she thought), but the voice of the paid soprano, the one brilliant space in the tedium. Something he found more beautiful than the stained-glass windows, the marble memorial plaques, the psalms. Launching into Mozart's *Alleluia* on Palm Sunday, *O Holy Night* on Christmas Eve, *Be Still, My Soul* on some less sacred day, Vincent would turn his head and regard her in the choir loft, high above him, against his mother's admonishings. You were supposed to pretend the voice came directly from God, the paid soprano a vessel of God's noise. You were not supposed to note her effort, imagine the sweat on her top lip, the phlegm in her cotton handkerchief.

He watched her in the choir loft, hands clasped tightly, eyes focused on some vanishing point on high, singing out over all of them. She was, in her isolation, magnificent.

The others, including his mother, called her dumpy, dowdy, and said she earned her living in the basement of Gimbel's. The $20 they gave her each Sunday, when she traveled on the ferry across the water, was more than enough – someone else would not charge. But, they agreed, they needed her.

Vincent noticed the contradiction in them.

Not even the sound of her voice could hold him.

Jimmy was a small man – 'dapper' was the word some used – Vincent, at seventeen, tall and broad as a swimmer, quiet for a boy. The man swam in the sports coat, but the mother did not ask Vincent if the sleeves might be shortened: that seemed to be going too far.

The boy did not hesitate to hand over the coat: he usually did as his mother asked, whether he wanted to or not. Neither mother nor son cared for confrontation. She had taught him that only 'low-class' people raised their voices, disagreed openly, caused 'scenes'. Born among such people, she wanted nothing more than to leave them behind – thought she had when she married Vincent's father.

And here she was, dating a man who didn't own a jacket, whose prized possession was a crazy mixed-up car. Her son kept mum.

'You can't judge a book by its cover,' she might say, not extending that charity to the paid soprano.

26

Vincent did own a blue serge suit, but his wrists extended way beyond the ends of the sleeves, and in it he looked like a Dead End kid dressed up. The sleeves had been let out as far as possible by the tailor in the shop downstairs, but no help. And besides, he had worn it to his father's funeral the year before, and it saddened his mother to see him in it. But she did not toss it away or give it to the Salvation Army. Now it hung in the back of the hall closet behind his father's World War II dress uniform, under a shelf that held a white wedding album with gold lettering, and a furrier's box containing ancient glassy-eyed stone martens. Signs of a person's history. Mementos.

They would never have said it to each other — not 'in so many words' — but each was relieved at the father's death. 'He's at peace now. He's out of pain,' was what she said.

He wasn't a falling-down drunk, or public embarrassment — not at first — just a man who dosed himself a few ounces each hour of each day. But soon his disability checks couldn't maintain his needs and he began to hock things (she must have redeemed the stone martens a dozen times if she'd redeemed them once) and, later, more desperate, to plead break-ins by large, dangerous Negroes, or hopped-up Puerto Ricans.

Soon, he was verging on public embarrassment. People pitied him when they saw him on the streets, weighed down like a peddler, as glassy-eyed as the stone martens draped around his neck. The cops at the local precinct thrilled to the idea of nabbing a few marauders — they'd been pouring onto the island ever since the bridge was opened — and were disappointed when the pawnbroker identified the plaintiff as the perpetrator. 'We'll let you off with a warning this time. Understand?'

Why did he drink? Misery. Oblivion — the need for. Something to do.

The usual.

His wife passed him off as a casualty of war. Wounded. Shell-shocked. Too genteel for his own good.

A man who had helped liberate Paris.

Actually his wound had been caused by a jeep accident. 'Just like Patton,' he joked with her when they first met.

In fact he'd never left Fort Dix. But he went along with her story; it was the least he could do. And when the minister and a few of the elders dropped by, he splashed some cold water on his face, sucked on a peppermint, and told them about weeping Frenchmen and girls craving nylons and children screaming for Hershey bars – just like in the movies. And he knew not a damned soul was fooled. Not for a minute.

They hardly spoke of him after he passed on.

Jimmy was grateful to have the loan of the sports coat and in return – for he was not a man to take something for nothing – offered Vincent driving lessons.

Jimmy's car in 1969 was too young to be classic and too old to be cool, but it had an individuality to be built upon, and he set about making it one of a kind. He had it painted and the seats recovered, the words AL'S DRIVING SCHOOL removed from one door, and CAUTION IS OUR MIDDLE NAME from the other. It became yellow, with red and black and green upholstery. Jimmy stood back: it looked 'jazzy'.

To his eye. 'One of a kind,' he repeated, while Vincent's mother hoped she could convince him to trade it in, or at least have it painted black, if they were to have any future together at all.

That was future. Fun, the here-and-now, was something else. And what she called her 'serious side' was quiet when she took her place in the death seat and worked her set of controls. Riding shotgun. Some Sundays after church she and Jimmy would compete against each other on the black gravel roads around Wolfe's Pond, roaring up and down, one accelerating while the other slammed the brake, black clouds rising, chasing them.

Careening past the edge of other people's picnics, skirting the Arthur Kill, around and around, out of breath, as if they were powering the car themselves.

'Wonder what your son would say if he could see you.'

'I'm still a young woman, you know. Not just someone's widowed mother.'

'I know.'

'This is where they shot part of *Splendor in the Grass*,' she told him, claiming fame. 'Ever see it?'

'I'm not much for the movies,' he answered, telling her something she already knew. He told her he was not a watcher; he was a man of action.

'Natalie Wood is a doll.' She closed the subject, and pressed hard on her gas pedal.

'Say,' he yelled over the roar of the Chevy.

'What?'

'Let's go over to Jersey.'

'What for?'

He spun them out of the park and onto Hylan Boulevard, passing the house where schoolchildren were taught year-in, year-out, Washington signed some papers, and then slept. To the Outerbridge Crossing, then down the Jersey shore.

The car in its original incarnation had been spotted by Jimmy on the Staten Island Ferry early one morning – on the *Mary Murray* to be precise, as Jimmy was whenever he told his story; one of the oldest vessels in the fleet, with a huge greased-over portrait of its namesake in the main salon opposite the steaming Sabrett's hot dogs in their glass case. The words under the painting told people that Mary Murray, who also gave her name to Murray Hill, held off a band of Red Coats during the Revolution – single-handed.

'I was standing there, having a cup of coffee,' Jimmy explained, 'when something told me to go below. You know those feelings you get?'

The car was at the foot of the stairs. He walked around it, just knew he wanted it, made an offer to the driver — who said he was Al's brother-in-law — and got it cheap.

It had potential, he said.

'You weren't afraid it was "hot"?' she asked him.

He didn't really care. 'You get a nose for these things,' he answered her. Why worry? He'd made the car his own. Not even its own mother would recognize it.

The two men clinched the deal below decks where cigarette smoke from commuters blocked any possibility of a sea breeze, but at least cut across the aroma of the garbage scows, plowing back and forth between Manhattan, Brooklyn, Jersey. The stench of Camels, Luckies, Winstons was surely better than the smell of decay: the mountains of bones, letters, tin cans, Kotex, left-over spaghetti, condoms, sour milk, razor blades, fetuses, party favors — all mingling on the flat-bottomed barges, passing in Dantesque procession to their dumping grounds.

The thick blue smoke of the cigarettes, even at eight in the morning, cast a romantic shadow. You could summon up the fog of a film set, and you could see Fred Astaire in *Shall We Dance*, singing to Ginger Rogers, 'They can't take that away from me'.

Vincent also knew the ferry. He went to school in the City — as island people called Manhattan — and took the boat every morning. Riding the waves, dodging the garbage barges, ice floes, tugs nudging a liner in or out, Vincent moved among the commuters, among the old Italian men barking 'Shine? Shine?', among the hair-netted counterwomen, weary, fresh, serving up coffee, Danish, among the oddballs lolling around the urinals. He walked the length and breadth of the boat, around the deck, watching the sooted skyscrapers coming closer, the open-ness of the harbor narrowing.

He usually ended up in the smokers' cabin, below decks, puffing a forbidden Lucky, listening to the talk around him while desperately trying to memorize a poem for the first period, English Lit. He sat among people he knew only by sight – the 7:45 was unvarying in its cargo – people he had been taught he was not a part of. He could put the book, the poem between them, protecting himself from them.

You could be sitting in a smoky, overheated, crowded cabin on a boat on the water and the life of your mind could keep you in total isolation.

'Quinquereme of Nineveh/ From distant Ophir,' he spoke in his head, certain that at that moment not another soul in the cabin, on the boat, was echoing him.

'Look up any unfamiliar words in the poem and be prepared to use them in a sentence,' had been the teacher's command.

He might make a joke of it. 'A quinquereme is a galley ship not unlike the Staten Island Ferry,' he might say. And the teacher would call him a smart aleck, and never suspect the poem had gotten to him.

And he'd grin in the back of the room, tilting his chair dangerously, while the rest of the IGC's sat straight, dull.

Maybe, maybe not.

His dreams were still fresh at this hour of the morning, sometimes stealing his attention from his homework, the people around him. He loved dreaming, loved the colors, the strangeness, the freedom of them. One he rehearsed over and over, sometimes excited by it; so excited that he had to snuff his Lucky and get out and move; sometimes he was ashamed. What would they think if he told them about the paid soprano and how he had fucked her in the back of Jimmy's Chevy? Would they be shocked at the fucking, or the fact that she was old enough to be his mother? *La vida es sueño y sueños sueños son.* Spanish class; fifth period. 'Tell me what does Calderon mean by this.' – another teacher's command.

When the fog enveloped all of them and the horns sounded their warning across the water, it could have been a scene from *Outward Bound*, and he might shudder if he thought

31

these people would be his company for all eternity. Or would he?

People laughed in the smoke one morning at a boy, about seventeen also, who asked, pleading with the commuting women (for on the early morning trips the boats held mostly women) to let him rub the high heels of their office shoes against his face. When the women refused, laughing, the boy retreated.

Vincent felt his face redden.

Voices, against the quarreling of seagulls thick after one of the scows, against the thumping pistons of the engine, raised in counterpoint.

'And he has such *nice* skin.'

'What does that have to do with it?'

'People like that usually have pimples.'

'How many people like that do you know?'

'I've lived.'

'Like the guy that killed those nurses?'

'Someone said that if they weren't nurses they wouldn't have died.'

'That's nuts.'

'There's always someone.'

'What do you mean?'

'Authorities, so-called.'

'I had enough of that shit when I was in school.'

'They said that they were trained to take care of people.'

'They were women, weren't they?'

'I'd pull the switch.'

Heads nodded. There was no verbal response to that — except: 'You said it.'

'But him,' someone said, meaning Vincent, 'he's an all-American boy.'

He tried not to hear, even as they commented on his build, his attention to his book, how he never bothered anyone.

Silence.

Then, soon enough, their talk turned elsewhere. Stories of the night before, predictions of the day to come. Who was getting married, when, and did they have the hall lined up. Puerto Rico as a honeymoon spot.

'It's really empty. Most of them are here.'

Bosses.

As they spoke, they smoked, sipped their coffee from cardboard containers with fanciful little boats drawn on them grabbed at the counter upstairs, or snatched on the run from the Commuter's Spa in the terminal; between the Food Farm where some of them would grab the makings for dinner on the way home, and the Normandy Bar & Grill, named by a man who had landed at Omaha Beach.

Between coffee and dinner was the day-at-the-office, where they were employed in companies clustered around Wall Street. High finance. Cargoes. Speculation. Import. Export. Banks. Stockbrokers. Shipping Lines. They were the women who answered the phones. Typed and typed and typed. Fluently decorated steno-pads with the grace of Pitman. The romance of capital, far-flung places, exotic teas and coffees, was lost on them. They sat in swivel chairs, wired to headsets. Ran errands. Welcomed clients. Ate their bag lunches in Trinity Churchyard in the shadow of Alexander Hamilton, or in Battery Park in the shadow of cannon, or splurged for a sandwich and coffee in Choc' Full o'Nuts.

Most of their husbands, were there husbands, did not travel by sea to their jobs. They were truck drivers, plumbers, pipefitters, mechanics, worked the docks. The fortunate ones were their own men. Others were stationed in Da Nang, and elsewhere. One man shared the sea with his wife – he was on a cruiser in the Gulf of Tonkin.

'Jesus, I wish I had a dollar for every time I passed that,' a woman said, as the Statue of Liberty or Ellis Island passed by: the hollow female, her cracked arm held aloft. The collection of red buildings, suggesting cavernous insides, echoes, pushing, shoving, people with tags tied to them, quarantine.

Many of these women lived in houses in which an old woman or an old man could recollect their first sight of either thing.

Almost every woman on the boat had someone in Vietnam, knew someone there, at least had a neighbor whose son, husband, nephew was way the hell across the world. One woman wore a watch in the shape of a beetle around her neck, sent from Saigon. She didn't regard the pickets around the recruiting office she had to walk by to get to work with kindness. She called them 'spoiled brats', and worse.

These were Vincent's shipmates.

At first Jimmy's presence didn't bother Vincent – he didn't let it bother him. His mother had been alone for a long time, even when his father was alive. But more and more they would take to her room, saying they were going to watch TV, locking the door – he could hear the skeleton key turn each time. He listened for it.

After each turning he felt his face go hot and a fury rose in him that was frightening. He had never been so angry before in his life. He didn't really understand it.

The fury invaded his dreams, interrupted them, so he no longer remembered them; just slivers of color remained. His encounter with the paid soprano vanished. His sleep was broken, and he woke exhausted.

In the morning her door would be ajar, and each morning he would push it in further, gently, not to wake her, not to say goodbye before running down the hill to the ferry, but to check. And seeing her alone, curled on one side, peaceful, eased his fury, and he wondered if he might have imagined the skeleton key turning the night before.

This slight doubt calmed him, but the calm did not last. He would find Jimmy's razor on the porcelain ledge above the sink, or a used coffee cup on the kitchen table. Who does

34

he think he is? He got hot all over again, slamming the front door, running down the stairs, down the side streets to the boat, feeling the cobblestones bruise his feet through his sneakers.

Son of a bitch! he yelped in the morning air.

She slept through his departure most mornings. If he woke her she put it down to his haste to get to school – they had told her he was an Intellectually Gifted Child, hadn't they? – and not miss the early boat, a boy's natural exhuberance. Especially a boy like him.

She rose slowly, showered, took coffee in her robe, switched on the Today show, tidied up the place, took something out of the freezer, then went to her job at the diner down the street where she worked the late-morning, early-afternoon shift.

With Jimmy around she was relieved of some of the financial terror she had known. He was generous; he paid his way, gave her money for groceries, towards the rent and utilities. That, and the money she got paid on her husband's death, made her almost a lady of leisure. At least she could relax. At least she no longer had to work two jobs, running from the diner to the public school, where she cleaned and polished banisters, steps, bathrooms.

Now that the diner was adding on she was going to be kicked upstairs, called 'hostess'; things were looking up.

As soon as she had some extra cash she was going to buy Vincent a graduation suit – from Barney's, in the City.

When he was not locked behind her door, Jimmy taught Vincent how to drive, trying to enter his life as a friend.

'I guess you miss your old man.'

Of course he didn't – he didn't miss the pretense, the covering up. The not-knowing what would be missing, what the poor slob had bartered away. 'I guess so.'

'Your mother says he was a hero in the war.'

'Yeah.'

'I would've loved to have been in that one.'

'How come you weren't?'

'Too young. You want to stop here for a beer?'

'My mother doesn't like me to drink.'

'C'mon. I won't tell if you won't. What she don't know won't hurt her.'

'You don't understand.'

'Understand?'

'My father had a problem. She's afraid. That's all.'

'I had an old man who drank and I'm just fine. But if you don't want to, you don't want to. Just decide for yourself. Be – ' he hesitated – oh, what the hell – 'a man.'

'Okay.' Vincent felt the fury beginning and quickly turned down the window, almost yanking the handle out of the door, begging the cold wind to take the heat away.

But it couldn't.

'I bet you weren't too young.' He had control of Jimmy's prized possession. 'I bet you were a faggot.'

'Watch it!' Gray water cascaded across the windshield.

Vincent tried to concentrate on the rutted street, doing his best to hit every puddle left from the rain of the night before.

'Hey! Watch it! I've got whitewalls, you know.'

'Okay,' he said. 'Okay, faggot,' he spoke to himself.

Vincent drove with deliberate caution after that, studiously avoiding every pothole and body of stale water.

'Okay,' Jimmy conceded. 'I get the message. I didn't mean to give advice. I know I ain't your old man. But don't you ever say that to me again or I'll knock your fucking teeth down your throat. I don't care if you're her son or not.'

'Sure.'

'I mean it.'

'I get the message.'

Vincent slowed the car almost to a stop. Jimmy gently lowered the accelerator on his side, floored it, while the boy struggled with the brake. Sailor's Snug Harbor flew by. Vincent was losing control.

36

'I'll show you who's boss.'

There was a sudden turn and the car skidded in the wet street. Feet lifted from the pedals in synchronicity and the car rolled to a stop outside the gypsum plant.

Vincent got out of the car.

They switched places silently; Jimmy took the wheel.

'Do you mind if I turn on the radio?'

'No,' Jimmy responded. 'Be my guest.'

Leaning forward the boy turned the knob of the radio and tuned to WINS. 'Give us twenty minutes and we'll give you the world.'

His mother seemed not to notice his elaborate sullen-ness whenever Jimmy was present. At least she never asked him, 'What's the matter?'

He had no one to talk to, and the fury was bearing down on him. The thing drove him. He had to move.

Each night, after the skeleton key turned, he would sneak out of his room in the dark apartment, sneak into the living room and find the porcelain dish on the coffee table where each night Jimmy deposited his keys and wallet. He slid the keys in one pocket and a few bills from the wallet into another.

'You want her, it'll cost you,' he whispered into the dark; the only other sound was the hum of the television from her room.

He'd crack open the front door, slide out, go down the stairs and find the car.

He drove and drove and drove. Sometimes straddling the hump in front and working both sets of controls, one foot playing chicken with the other. 'Gas father, brake mother; brake father, gas mother.' Back and forth, back and forth. Was this hate?

He'd drive up to the parking lot at Silver Lake and regard the steamed-up windows of the cars, laughing when the cops rolled in and flashlights were pointed, played over crotches, faces, warnings given.

Maybe if he had a girl?

Maybe he should see the minister and – what? Confess to what?

Once, he drove the full length of Victory Boulevard on the passenger side, steering with one hand out of view, honking the horn so people would think he was the captive of a ghost-driver.

No cops came.

He ended each night at a car wash, scrubbing the precious whitewalls so he wouldn't be found out. Wishing he could run through the jets and brushes himself.

Of course he was caught.

Jimmy could let the missing cash, the rising odometer, go only so far.

One morning before church he confronted Vincent.

'I know you've been using my car without asking.'

'And you've been using my mother without asking.'

Jimmy was no match for him. The little man drew his right hand back and Vincent only laughed at him, skirted the chair that separated them, and ran out the door.

'Where's Vincent?' His mother was making the final arrangement of her Sunday veil.

'How should I know? He's your kid.'

'Did something happen?'

'No.'

They walked to church that morning.

What happened that Sunday morning was the talk of the boat on Monday.

'Jeez, just like Chappaquiddick.'

Not exactly.

He revved the engine of the yellow car and ran it full force against the gate. At the last second, like James Dean in *Rebel*

Without a Cause, he rolled out of the driver's side, rolling until he came to a stop in a pile of ropes used to secure the boat to its berth. The car's ass stuck up in the air, then slid rapidly down into the green-gray, like the *Titanic*.

The few people below decks that Sunday were sitting in their cars, snoozing off a hangover from the City or reading the papers. No one noticed him in his pile of ropes. Eyes rose from papers, woke from dozes at the sound of the gate breaking, not giving, and watched Jimmy's 'Yellow Peril' sink to its watery grave.

Vincent found himself at the Seaman's Mission, was given Sunday dinner, pulled on a bottle of wine offered by one of the guests, slept in a green-blanketed cot. Slept through the night and into the next morning, when he strolled to the recruiting office near the Battery.

PART TWO

A Hanged Man

This story is based on two historical details. The first is the suicide of a man who hanged himself from his whipping post in a building used for the punishment of slaves. Such whipping houses — removed from the plantations — were not uncommon in the years immediately preceding the Civil War, when abolitionists, in groups, came south to investigate reports of the mistreatment of slaves.

The second detail is the life of a man named Peg-leg Joe, a one-legged sailor (we do not know if Joe was black or white or Indian — or a combination thereof), who led slaves to freedom from as far away as Mobile, Alabama. The following verse from an American folk song is one of the only reports we have of Peg-leg Joe: 'De riva's bank am a very good road/ De dead trees show de way/ Lef' foot, peg foot goin' on/ Foller de drinkin' gourd.'

There is a clearing in the woods. A heavy rain has fallen the night before. Water stands around the foundation of a building in the clearing, seeping into brick. The slate roof is washed clean, shingles glint in the early summer sun.

A brick walkway in the form of a cross leads to the front door of the building. It is lined on every side with roses, begun with caution and formality, now loosed, each challenging the fitness of the other; thorns from one cane cut into the cane of another, drawing blood. Musk, Damask, Isfahan, Old Blush, captured on trails blazed by Crusaders, wild scents flashing in the clearing, fetid, fleshy, sweet. An archway of Persian lilac cascades around the entrance to the building.

To the side, by itself, is the sport of the Apothecary, Rosa Mundi, her striped red over pink ground; red from her parent, the rose of Lancaster, about which every schoolchild in those days knew.

The building began life as a station, set in the middle of nowhere, beyond the trees and fields pertinent to the town. *Began life* is not quite right, since the place never actually came to life. Set at the end of a failed spur line where daytrippers had been meant to disembark, admire the roses, the design of the place. Visions of country excursions with parasoled ladies in tasseled carriages held together by chains fell flat. Baskets of sweetmeats and biscuits and chicken legs went unpacked. Jugs of syllabub unpoured. The place seemed too far, not far enough, from home. These people not suited to day trips. The spur line in the end was impractical, not suited to any real cargo.

Now, a slender minaret – exotic doodad embellishing the delicate structure – poked up, brushing against the budding branch of an oak. On one balcony a pair of mockingbirds fought and sang, with more repertoire than a muezzin ever had.

The whole establishment became a sort of shame. A waste. Good money poured out. Almost a complete disgrace until someone suggested another use and saved the town's face – in more ways than one.

The building was well-suited to its new found purpose – its setting in a clearing in the woods beyond the town was exactly what was needed, and the architect, dead and gone, was praised as a man of foresight.

Albeit one with a taste for what one town father called the 'Byzantine', referring not only to the minaret, the roses known to Saladin, but to the plaster replica of Powers's *Greek Slave*, set on a pedestal in the waiting room, all the rage at the Crystal Palace, the architect had patiently explained.

Noise could not travel to town from this place. Visitors suspect nothing. Sensibilities spared.

No one would hear a thing. Not even the Powhatan with his ear to the iron rail.

Anyway the rail had been torn up, interrupted. The Powhatan long gone.

The only ones to hear would be the ones waiting their turn. That was not a bad thing.

He was facing west. Rivers. Smokies. Expanse. Prairie. Monuments.

Behind him was the ocean. Traders. Clippers. One point of a triangle. Cotton. Tobacco.

These were at his back.

He was hanging motionless. Drab. Drab in his work-clothes. Gray. Brown spots where blood had dried. Hands hung at his sides. Eyes stared. He was rigid. Stiff. Dead weight. Tongue swollen and thick in his mouth.

Beneath him sawdust covered the floor. Stained and wet, it had not been changed in some time. At his side, within arm's reach, were that not absurd, was a rack which held his tools. Cat-o-nine. Rope. Bull. Each suspended by a hand-carved handle, smoothed by sweat and use.

He might hang there for days. Not be found until someone had need of him, his craft. He had no people of his own.

Sunlight passing through the minaret illumined him. Mockingbirds fought above him, then burst into song. Would they swoop down and peck out his eyes?

Early summer. Buds heavy.

The time of the year when Yankees thawed and headed south to investigate. Poking and probing into the 'wrongs', the inquisitive little bands were well-received. (To be impolite would be impolitic.)

Returning home to their mills and factories and righteous societies, their girl-workers twisting filaments on looms, living, if you could call it that, jammed in bleak white-washed rooms, fighting damp and cold – and dust. Clinging to eyebrows, lids, lips, skin whitened, chest heavy – the cotton dust was everywhere, was in the air when Whittier came to speak. Eyes watered.

But they can at least read, a visitor might say. Our nigras, the host might reason, have at least the sun.

Now just where did those Yankees reckon the cotton on those looms came from?

India? Egypt?

Blest be the tie that binds, the thread of connection.

Right now, at this very moment, as this hanging man waited on discovery, soul God knows where, if, evensong was being sung in the stone church, for the benefit of women in black and men in black, unused to such elaborate service, severe and shunning any excess.

'To our distinguished visitors,' the pastor spoke, 'brothers and sisters, welcome.'

He paused. 'Let us pray.'

Then:

> *My soul be on thy guard, Ten thousand foes arise;*
> *The hosts of sin are pressing hard To draw thee from*
> *the skies.*
> *O watch and fight and pray; The battle ne'er give o'er;*
> *Renew it boldly every day, And help divine implore.*

Each recognized the song as theirs. Weighed down by righteousness, they sang their hearts out.

But one woman, black taffeta under a stained-glass window, who wished for something gentler.

After the service there was a somber and sedate dinner, with Bible readings, pan-roasted oysters, watermelon pickle, meat cut high off the hog. A pale old man standing in the shadow of the breakfront, silver salver at the ready. Darkness masking the line running from his eyelid to his jawbone. A lady tinkled Mozart on a spinet.

Over port and cigars the visiting men – the ladies had taken their leave, even now were being helped into their night-things, awkwardly, by women who did not speak, did not respond to them – the men were left the delicate questions, the thing they had come all this way to probe.

Upstairs a woman cries out, seized with gripes, wondering if the stories about poisoning are true. Ashamed for wondering. We are their friends, she says to herself, not knowing these dark silent women at all. Don't they realize that? The trichina worms its way into her muscle. She muffles her cry. She lies back in the featherbed, praying for the pain to pass, not wanting to wander around this house, huge and dark, in search of help.

Downstairs the conversation, inquisition, continues.
We have heard . . .
Sir, I beg you . . .
Of brutality . . . branding
Consider your sources . . .
Iron necklaces . . .
Sir, would you wilfully . . .
An excess of punishment . . .
Damage . . .
There are reports . . .
Something on which your livelihood depends?
No.
Well, sir.
We have heard of the lightening of the Africans . . .
Much exaggerated . . .
Their skin . . .
You and your companions . . .
The pale old man, right eye droopy as he tires, as the line to his jawbone tugs at him, pours port.

Are most welcome to look into any nook and cranny on
this farm.
Or mine. Or mine. Or mine.
The chorus chimes in.

The company adjourns. The old man replaces the decanter
in the breakfront. Thinks again and pours himself a glass.
Drinks. Then marks the level on the crystal for the mistress
to note where the gentlemen left it. He regards the ruby
liquid, himself in it, the line which pains him, then snuffs the
candlelight.

Near dawn the figure stiffer than before. A rat sniffs at the
leg of the upended stool, moving on to nibble at the dangling
thongs. The wind through the minaret imitates human
sounds.

The sideboard creaks from the weight of meat. All is laid out
in silver. Silver is set on white linen which covers the fine
veneer of mahogany. The same pale old man stands against
the wall.

The stench of dead humanity is high. The rat has made her
way across the floor to where the salt is kept. She licks at the
crystals.

All hell breaks loose at breakfast. Well, at least temporarily.
Temporarily, good manners are suspended. Tempers, held
tight last night, loosed. All because a visitor raises the
question of Mrs Stowe and her Uncle Tom.
The host explodes. Melodrama! Sheer melodrama! Written
by a homely woman to buy a black silk dress.
There is silence at the table.
Upstairs a woman vomits into a silk pillowslip.

A young woman is standing outside the door of the station,
a slip of paper in her hand. She is too frightened to care

about the roses. She has not been here before but knows too well the stories. She wears an apron on which she has appliquéd figures, as if they will protect her. Jonah in the belly of the beast. Keep her company. The women at the foot of the cross. Remind her that this life is not all. Shàngó aloft, riding a chariot. Swing low.

She knocks. Loud. Then louder.

Please, marster, don't prolong my agony.

She does not dare turn the knob.

She cannot look through the windows. They are painted black.

She slides the slip of paper underneath the door.

Cap'n: fifty lashes and charge to account.

She sits on a stump to wait.

She sat there for a long time and the door did not open; no one else appeared. In her entire life she had never had this much time when she had been completely alone, not called on. But anticipating punishment robbed her of the use of solitude; she was only frightened.

The fright built in her over the hours, the tension in her pitching so high that her ears began to ring, and she felt she would explode unless she could move. So she got up and began to walk around, more to relieve her terror than for any other reason.

At first she explored the grounds, trying to ease her mind with the smell and color of roses. Trying to trace the red stripes of the flesh of one she was only reminded of the stripes awaiting her, which would make ditches across her back.

The only interruption in the stillness was birdsong, and she tried to follow the changes of the two mockingbirds atop the building's tower. Listening, she walked back and forth on the path, toes tracing the moss between the brick. Soon this was as bad as sitting on a stump – she turned to walk away.

Running did not enter her mind; she began to walk away.

When she had walked as long as she had spent by that blasted, haunted building she had the nerve to look behind her, and ahead of her, to her left and to her right. Behind and ahead were woods; to her right, woods. To her left she sensed running water and turned to walk towards it.

It was too sweet. Soaking her feet in this rushing, cold water. Concealed by woods, not a soul to hear her. No break in the stillness here but the breaking of water on rock. She grabbed a bunch of cress from the riverbank and let her mouth enjoy its heat. A cold, wide river was at her side, running — daring her: escape! Bless me, Oshun, she prayed to the *orisha* of sweet water. With that prayer she cast her lot.

She got up, wiped her mouth with the corner of her apron, and walked on. She looked down at the muddy bank and recognized the trace of a track: a human foot beside the circle of a peg-leg. The mark of the journey-man. Spying this she walked forward. There was another track, then another, and after a hundred such tracks she was able to breathe deep, and take heart in this other human presence.

A Woman Who Plays Trumpet Is Deported

This story is dedicated to the memory of Valaida Snow, trumpet-player, who was liberated – or escaped – from a concentration camp. She weighed sixty-five pounds. She died in 1956 of a cerebral hemorrhage. This was inspired by her story, but it is an imagining.

She came to me in a dream and said: 'Girl, you have no idea how tough it was. I remember once Billie Holiday was lying in a field of clover. Just resting. And a breeze came and the pollen from the clover blew all over her and the police came out of nowhere and arrested her for possession.'

'And the stuff was *red* . . . it wasn't even white.'

A woman. A black woman. A black woman musician. A black woman musician who plays trumpet. A bitch who blows. A lady trumpet-player. A woman with chops.

It is the thirties. She has been fairly successful. For a woman, black, with an instrument not made of her. Not made of flesh but of metal.

Her father told her he could not afford two instruments for his two children and so she would have to learn her brother's horn.

This woman tucks her horn under her arm and packs a satchel and sets her course. Paris first.

This woman flees to Europe. No, *flee* is not the word. Escape? Not quite right.

She wants to be let alone. She wants them to stop asking for vocals in the middle of a riff. She wants them to stop

55

calling her *novelty, wonder*, chasing after her orchid-colored Mercedes looking for a lift. When her husband gets up to go, she tosses him the keys, tells him to have it washed every now and then, the brass eyeballs polished every now and then — reminds him it's unpaid for and wasn't her idea anyway.

She wants a place to practice her horn, to blow. To blow rings around herself. So she blows the USA and heads out. On a ship.

And this is not one of those I'm travelin'-light-because-my-man-has-gone situations — no, that mess ended a long time before. He belongs in an orchid-colored Mercedes — although he'll probably paint the damn thing gray. It doesn't do for a man to flaunt, he would say, all the while choosing her dresses and fox furs and cocktail rings.

He belongs back there; she doesn't.

The ship is French. Families abound. The breeze from the ocean rosying childish cheeks, as uniformed women stand by, holding shuttlecocks, storybooks, bottles. Women wrapped in tricolor robes sip bouillion. Men slap cues on the shuffle-board court, disks skimming the polished deck. Where — and this is a claim to fame — Josephine Baker once walked her ocelot or leopard or cheetah.

A state of well-being describes these people, everyone is groomed, clean, fed. She is not interested in them, but glad of the calm they convey. She is not interested in looking into their staterooms, or their lives, to hear the sharp word, the slap of a hand across a girl's mouth, the moans of intimacy.

The ship is French. The steward assigned to her, Senegalese.

They seek each other out by night, after the families have retired. They meet in the covered lifeboats. They communicate through her horn and by his silver drum.

He noticed the horn when he came the very first night at sea to turn down her bed. Pointed at it, her. The next morning introduced her to his drum.

The horn is brass. The drum, silver. Metal beaten into memory, history. She traces her hand along the ridges of silver – horse, spear, warrior. Her finger catches the edge of a breast; lingers. The skin drumhead as tight as anything.

In the covered lifeboats by night they converse, dispersing the silence of the deck, charging the air, upsetting the complacency, the well-being that hovers, to return the next day.

Think of this as a reverse middle passage.

Who is to say he is not her people?

Landfall.

She plays in a club in the Quartier Latin. This is not as simple as it sounds. She got to the club through a man who used to wash dishes beside Langston Hughes at Le Grand Duc who knew a woman back then who did well who is close to Bricktop who knows the owner of the club. The trumpet player met the man who used to wash dishes who now waits tables at another club. They talked and he said, 'I know this woman who may be able to help you.' Maybe it was simple, lucky. Anyway, the trumpet player negotiated the chain of acquaintance with grace; got the gig.

The air of the club is blue with smoke. Noise. Voices. Glasses do clink. Matches and lighters flare. The pure green of absinthe grows cloudy as water is added from a yellow ceramic pitcher.

So be it.

She lives in a hotel around the corner from the club, on the rue de l'Université. There's not much to the room: table, chair, bed, wardrobe, sink. She doesn't spend much time there. She has movement. She walks the length and breadth of the city. Her pumps crunch against the gravel paths in the parks. Her heels click along the edge of the river. All the time her mind is on her music. She is let alone.

She takes her meals at a restaurant called Polidor. Her food is set on a white paper-covered table. The lights are bright. She sits at the side of a glass-fronted room, makes friends with a waitress and practices her French. *Friends* is too strong; they talk. Her horn is swaddled in purple velvet and rests on a chair next to her, next to the wall. Safe.

Of course, people stare occasionally, those to whom she is unfamiliar. Once in a while someone puts a hand to a mouth to whisper to a companion. Okay. No one said these people were perfect. She is tired – too tired – of seeing the gape-mouthed darky advertising *Le Joyeux Nègre*. Okay? Looming over a square by the Panthéon in all his happy-go-luckiness.

While nearby a Martiniquan hawked *L'Étudiant Noir*.

Joyeux Négritude.

A child points to the top of his *crème brulée* and then at her, smiles. Okay.

But no one calls her nigger. Or asks her to leave. Or asks her to sit away from the window at a darker table in the back by the kitchen, hustling her so each course tumbles into another. *Crudités* into *timbale* into *caramel*.

This place suits her fine.

The piano player longs for a baby part-*Africaine*. She says no. Okay.

They pay her to play. She stays in their hotel. Eats their food in a clean, well-lighted place. Pisses in their toilet.

No strange fruit hanging in the Tuileries.

She lives like this for a while, getting news from home from folks who pass through. Asking, 'When you coming back?'

'Man, no need for that.'

Noting that America is still TOBA (tough on black asses), lady trumpet players still encouraged to vocalize, she remains. She rents a small apartment on Montparnasse, gets a cat, gives her a name, pays an Algerian woman to keep house.

All is well. For a while.

1940. The club in the Quartier Latin is shut tight. Doors

boarded. The poster with her face and horn torn across. No word. No word at all. Just murmurs.

The owner has left the city on a freight. He is not riding the rails. Is not being chased by bad debts. He is standing next to his wife, her mother, their children, next to other women, their husbands, men, their wives, children, mothers-in-law, fathers, fathers-in-law, mothers, friends.

The club is shut. This is what she knows. But rumors and murmurs abound.

The piano player drops by the hotel, leaves a note. She leaves Paris. She heads north.

She gets a gig in Copenhagen, standing in for a sister moving out – simple, lucky – again. Safe. Everyone wore the yellow star there – for a time.

1942. She is walking down a street in Copenhagen. The army of occupation picks her up. Not the whole army – just a couple of kids with machine guns.

So this is how it's done.

She found herself in a line of women. And girls. And little children.

The women spoke in languages she did not understand. Spoke them quietly. From the tone she knew they were encouraging their children. She knows – she who has studied the nuance of sound.

Her horn tucked tight under her armpit. Her only baggage.

The women and girls and little children in front of her and behind her wore layers of clothing. It was a warm day. In places seams clanked. They carried what they could on their persons.

Not all spoke. Some were absolutely silent. Eyes moved into this strange place.

Do you know the work of Beethoven?

She has reached the head of the line and is being addressed by a young man in English. She cannot concentrate. She sweats through the velvet wrapped around her horn. All around her women and girls and little children – from which she is apart, yet of – are being taken in three different directions. And this extraordinary question.

A portrait on a schoolteacher's wall. Of a wiry-haired, beetle-browed man. And he was a colored genius, the teacher told them, and the children shifted in their seats.

Telemann? He wrote some fine pieces for the horn.

The boy has detected the shape of the thing under her arm. She stares and does not respond. How can she?

The voices of women and girls and little children pierce the summer air as if the sound was being wrenched from their bodies. The sun is bright. Beads of sweat gather at the neck of the young man's tunic.

It should not be hot. It should be drear. Drizzle. Chill. But she knows better. The sun stays bright.

In the distance is a mountain of glass. The light grazes the surface and prisms split into color.

Midden. A word comes to her. The heaps of shells, bones and teeth. Refuse of the Indians. The mound-builders. That place by the river just outside of town – filled with mystery and childhood imaginings.

A midden builds on the boy's table, as women and girls and little children deposit their valuables.

In the distance another midden builds.

Fool of a girl, she told herself. To have thought she had seen it all. Left it – the worst piece of it – behind her. The body burning – ignited by the tar. The laughter and the fire. And her inheriting the horn.

PART THREE

American Time, American Light

*A*s the leaves thinned the days shortened and the winter light cast everything cold. As the cold advanced quiet became the village – all sound was muffled. But for the fingers of ice cracking like gunshots in the night when the tree branches could no longer bear the weight of frozen water.

A lake formed in a valley, soft hills ringing around it. In these hills the forest waited. Beyond the homes of summer people, boarded and shrouded in winter; beyond the hill towns named Florida and Peru (with a long *e*) and Baptist Corner; beyond the churches, some abandoned, doors flung wide, molded ceilings scrolled and curlicued, chipped and darkened here and there; beyond the shops laying bare the artifacts of spinners and weavers and printers and merchants, decaled and prettified; beyond those spindles and spools and moveable type and adding machines; beyond the spruced, converted factories sporting cool cellars and underdone meat; beyond the deserted academies where dissenters sent their sons, strains of the Faith burgeoning, the sons soon giving, heading West to new terrain and wild naive flocks, excitement fit to burst; beyond the remains of spas, once gay, water flowing like there was no tomorrow, ladies sunk in porcelain tubs, breasts covered by a square of Irish linen by an Irish maid, good for what ails you; beyond the long, plain tobacco barns, green leaves browning, hung by Micmacs down from Nova Scotia; beyond the long green porch of the Independent Order of Scalpers, Narragansett on tap; beyond the ancient lilacs, French and English, some woman's pride and joy way back then; beyond the mounds stark, shards, bones, beads, unearthed, encrusted, feathers molted, gracing a vitrine in a county seat museum, legend typed on a manual with a chipped *t*; beyond a diorama in the same museum, class project of an eighth grade, settlers, miniature iron pot swinging over a blazing cardboard hearth, hasty pudding, silhouette cut from red construction paper, peeking through a cellophane window; beyond the libraries, Webster and Britannica, *Poor Boys Who Became Famous* and *Girls Who Made Good*, Olive Higgins Prouty and the *Christian Science Monitor*, benefactor smiling from the wall; beyond LIVE DEER, PETRIFIED CREATURES, NIGHT-CRAWLERS; beyond the hiding-places of slaves (still-secret), the homestead of W.E.B. DuBois, the dining room where Mumbet served the table, tin ceiling curling from artificial heat; beyond the meeting-places of Abolitionists, the collisions of Douglass and Brown and Phillips and Truth – beyond all this human interruption, this stopping and starting – memory, relic – the forest waited patiently to return, as it had done before and before.

In spaces between birch and pine and maple, soft indentations marked a cellar hole. A forsythia strained near where a porch had been. Stone steps, mossed and cracked, went nowhere. In the dark of the cellar hole, a wreck of a stove lay, its place of origin – FLORENCE – embossed on its oven door.

Potatoes – all eyes – seeded themselves in the soft black of the forest floor, and Vietnam veterans, alive in this dark, abandoned space, had found them. Underground springs lay frozen in wait, to explode into freshets. The movement of worms in the earth was suspended. Fish slept. Cress would grow thick and green once the water flowed.

You might live off the land, and water.

Middle-aged men, stubbled and yellowed, camped out, making do with potatoes, beer bought from the nearest Mini-Mart – where a cat named Mama-San prowled – and grass dried over the last summer.

A man named Frank nested in an overgrown dooryard.

Black Minorcas (once the rage – 'prolific layers of an extremely large egg') long absent. Packed squawking into a wagon headed West, amid bedclothes, irons, seed corn. The farm had failed; the family abandoned it – in 1895. With their children, those surviving, the mother and father crossed to Nebraska. Two pieces of granite marked the remains of two boys lost to measles.

Almost a century gone and no one had come to claim the land.

Frank felt in this deserted place, hidden and dark, as the last survivor – of he knew not what. The man who wakes up after the bombs have gone off? The one standing after a duel in a missile silo? The man the earth swallows, then vomits up? War? History? Family? His own life?

Survival, he knew, was not what it was cracked up to be – you bet your life.

He had no company, no spirit guides, not much of anything. He was alone. And glad of it. And scared of it.

Elsewhere men gathered together, and not to ask the Lord's blessing. 'Misery loves company,' his mother might have said – in her way capturing the human condition – and he wondered where that sudden recollection of her words had come from; his mind was practically wiped clean of memory.

'Not quite a *tabula rasa*,' the smartass VA doctor had said, 'but almost.'

At least Frank could remember to say 'Fuck you'.

Frank kept to himself, even at the hospital.

On his way to his nest he had stumbled on a group, sitting around a fire, drinking beer in the freezing cold. He quickly pulled back, to the edge of their circle. They took little notice. They were drinking and talking and smoking. Blue and gray wisps wreathed each of them, converging into a nimbus, traces of fire, cigarettes, joints, their own warm breath hitting the frigid air.

One of them wore a doughboy's hat and offered Frank a Bud. 'Here, man, take it.' He did, and began to retreat.

'Hey, later!' someone yelled after him.

All quiet on the western Mass. front. Little flashes. The lost boys. Little flashes. Robin Hood's Merry Men. Little flashes, lights in his miserable old head.

Looking over his shoulder he saw their firelight at the pinpoint center of their circle; the red of the fire against their camouflage and olive drab, and the white of the landscape, and the gray sentinels of bare trees. Nimbus drawing them together, blessing them.

Now, in the dooryard, he looked around. Everywhere the forest masked humanity. A hundred yards beyond the dooryard did not exist. He had no idea how to find the circle again.

He wanted only to stay in this place now he had found it, settle, wrap the wreck around him. He had done nothing wrong.

He was a 41-year-old man. He had walked away from somewhere he did not belong. Where the air was black with smoke, and blue from other men's misery, and flickering from the infernal light of the television.

What made him leave?

It just got to be too much.

In the dead of night he opened the footlocker under his bed and slid into his fatigues under the thin blanket. They hung on him and he felt like a kid trying on his father's clothes. His body was wasted, from too much smoke and not enough food. His chest caved and he could trace the bones in his pelvis. He had to move deliberately because his thoughts swirled and did not follow. He had to will himself – to dress, get up, sneak past, out, away. Down in the lobby, walls decorated with murals of the Lafayette Escadrille, a dim light barely illumined the desk of a night watchman, away from his post. Across from the desk, under a painting of an aircraft spiraling to earth, was an exhibit set up by the local historical society: CONTAGIOUS DISEASES IN NEW ENGLAND. A child's contagious bed, iron rectangle with barred sides, receptacle of nightmare, was the centerpiece of the exhibit and in the dim light from the desk it cast a huge shadow against the mural, bisecting the plane. 'They get you coming and going,' Frank whispered to himself, and began a soundless laugh.

A mannequin of a nurse, crisp and white and capped, stood to one side of the empty bed, pointing a plastic finger, fake mouth smiling into the emptiness. He started at the ghost, fought a desire to look up her skirt; he laughed again, knowing she would be as unreal, as ill-defined as the inflatable woman who made the rounds upstairs.

He fell to his belly, moved past the angel of mercy, and out of the lobby. He reached his right hand up to the knob of the front door, slid out, away.

He made his way up 1-91 on foot, in stealth. One foot in front of the other, one foot in front of the other. At a rest-stop he poked through the top layer of a dumpster. Hungry now, cold, he finished off a stranger's Big Mac which had been barely touched. 'You deserve a break today,' a TV chorus echoed. And he sang it into the cold night. He wished he had a flashlight and could search the dumpster – who knows what he might find? The wind hit at his ears and he seized a newspaper from the top of the trash and made himself a hat. He walked on, looking like an overgrown boy playing soldier; all he needed was a wooden sword. Hayfoot, strawfoot, hayfoot, strawfoot, he repeated to himself, to the frozen landscape, as he made his way away.

Sitting there, in his nest, he suddenly remembered, he who was not supposed to remember, in a little flash, suddenly and clearly, with a clarity of glass, a book he had loved as a boy, when books were his solitary, constant, comfort.

He could not conjure the title, did not expect to, but saw a picture – the cover – as if he held it in his hands. A boy in blue jeans and a white T-shirt. A bridge is in the background,

69

massive against the boy's slender body; the boy has walked across the bridge from one part of the city to another. The glint of a steel key is at the boy's feet. The picture begins to move. The boy picks up the key and wanders over to the pier of the bridge, as thick and as gray as an elephant's foot. Set into the pier is a heavy fire-door. The key fits and opens to a clean room. Small. Cot made with white sheets and a green wool blanket. One pillow. A table in the room, with a chair that slides under it. A stall shower and toilet off to one side. This might seem to be a cell but for the key. All a body needs. A room prepared for a caretaker or watchman but it is not in use. Someone has forgotten about it.

The boy in the book, in flight from home, has found a home. He moves in, gets a job in a supermarket, buys a hotplate, gets a library card.

He is on his own.

He must have been sixteen when he read that book, maybe younger. Who is he to say? Finding it on one of his weekly treks to the branch library. He was working his way through the books and away from his parents' wars.

Lying on his bed, or on the grass under the fire escape, his forefinger holding the place, looking, again studying the book itself. Then turning back to the page, the words and the sentences – the life of it. Trying to shut out the world while the world is exercising its influence – birdsong, a parent's voice, traffic noise, the smell of cooking, shouts at a pick-up game.

He was the boy who read. And it came to him now, in his nest, that the reading muscle had been severed and replaced by a plastic shunt.

He savored the picture of the boy, the room. Nothing else came. Surely it had been only a book? Only? Read a book and you will never be lonely. Who said that?

He sat back on the hard earth and the cold began to seep into him. He worked his way into the failed farmhouse. Beams blocked him and he was afraid to budge them and have the place cave in on him. Afraid to make a noise — why? There was no one to hear. He worked his way under the beams, on his belly, across someone else's kitchen floor, his face flat against flagstone — ice, ice cold.

He will find what the family has left behind.

A blue-backed speller is visible across the floor. Snow, ice, dapple the surface. Snow and ice are over everything. Snow and ice cover the brown remains of a newspaper under a crashed beam. The black of the type emerges through the white and against the brown. He traces the type with the forefinger of his right hand. Nothing makes sense.

United Opinion Erisypelas Bright's Disease Heart Failure THE ONLY SUBSTITUTE FOR MOTHER'S MILK Croup Eczema Diphtheria LIFE SENTENCE FOR STEALING BACON Ovarian Neuralgia Gout Scrofula LUCY CHILDS HAD A SHOCK LAST WEEK SO THAT SHE IS UNABLE TO SPEAK. IT IS WITH GREAT REGRET THAT WE CHRONICLE THE SAD NEWS Chautauqua Circle THE TRAINS ARE AGAIN DRAPED IN MOURNING ON ACCOUNT OF THE ACCIDENT ON THE SOUTH-BOUND MAIL WHEN AN ENGINEER AND A FIREMAN WERE KILLED Dr LeSure's Magic Compound Drs Starkey and Palen's Compound Oxygen Dr Keneally's Favorite Remedy Electric Bitters Hood's Sarsaparilla Blood Purifier Pain Balm OSCAR WILDE ON TRIAL Ripans Tabules THE LISTERS ARE BUSY TRYING TO SURPRISE PEOPLE BY APPEARING UNEXPECTEDLY Green Mountain Sarsaparilla Recommended by the Clergy 'I am a well man today and weigh 200 pounds' Lydia E Pinkham 'Young girls must know that self-preservation is the first law of nature' ROADS IMPASSABLE.

His eyes brush against the type. Nothing. He picks up the sheet and it flakes in his hands. Carefully he puts the bits in his breastpocket.

If he goes to sleep, he will not wake.

He sits back. Pulls the newspaper hat down so that the

paper brushes the bridge of his nose. Words are folded into each other.

He closes his eyes.

Some children were gathered at a creek. Boys and girls. On the shore lay a magnificent fish, scales rainbow in the light. A small boy is watching as it writhes in the stones and the dirt. He bends over, squeezes its middle and a mustard yellow ooze comes out. The children laugh. A girl moves forward and plays her finger through the ooze. The waters are rushing. A boy bites into the fish on a dare. The fish moves its mouth open and shut, open and shut, gasping, a place in its side, from the boy's teeth, leaks. Shoes are caked with mud, gathered around the daring boy, the fish.

The thaw, the spring, is on.

The black ink of the type from the newspaper hat runs down his cheeks, streaking him like war paint.

The children find him.

Burning Bush

*L*ast summer the forest shuddered as a Winnebago passed through, obscured by foolish fire.

The paper blazed a headline in Second Coming type – ELDER SISTER MISSING: POLICE FEAR FOUL PLAY – starker, darker than the one the day before.

The missing sister was a 75-year-old odd quantity, so people thought. Not someone anyone really knew, certainly harmless enough. Who would want to hurt such a little old lady? A rounded little woman with a covered head and soft brown coat who walked up and down the main street of the village, eager to speak with almost anyone, whom a few remembered as a strapping girl.

As she walked, casting a shadow, in line with the season, in line with the time of day, she remembered the events of her life and what she had come to.

One stood out: being taken to a sideshow at the tri-county fair when her father was alive. Where for a dime – when a dime meant something – you could peer at the freaks.

Why did people dress up their little children and march them handheld tight into the dark world of those deformities and dishonesties, for some of them were not to be believed, the sun hidden by the canvas of the circus tent, sawdust wet and sticking to black shoes like at a butcher's shop. Surely there was a space for those people – the genuine ones, the fakes were another matter – out West (Wyoming? Utah? Badlands? Black Hills?) where Sister told them a place had been found by a Dominican with sympathies for the misshapen.

Ahead of them in the darkness a tall man with a stovepipe hat named Doc welcomed the visitors – step right up, step right up. Was he the physician in charge? Behind him, lined side by side on a raised platform, were the gaudy freaks. Tattooed Lady. Smallest Mother in the World. Black Lobster Man. White Penguin Boy. Alligator Woman. Just there. See me. Two-faced Man. Woman with a leg growing from her armpit, her wedding ring brightly displayed, two-legged children at her side. Look at me. Armless, legless poet, a trunk of a girl penning verse with a contraption fixed to her tongue. Regard me.

And the main attraction, the reason so many dimes shone in the collection plate held by Doc's spangled assistant, sat above this chorus on a throne of bamboo and feathers and soft red cloth. The Girl from Martinique, born in slavery, so the legend read, for these people did not speak, did not announce themselves. And no one seemed to mind, or even notice, that slavery had ended in Martinique almost a hundred years before. But few if any in this landscape of skunk cabbage and fiddleheads and birches shaped like corkscrews and rock-bearing fields had even heard of such a place. Did they eat one another?

Never mind. The Girl from Martinique was a sight all right and well worth the price of admission. A piece of cloth wrapped her breasts and wound itself behind her, crossing her body beneath her navel. She was uncovered for the most part, for she was *parti-colored*, so read the legend, as if you had to be told, had to have it pointed out to you, and this was her uniqueness. Patches of black bumped against ivory. *This checkerboard of a woman owes her skin to certain practices of her native land brought with her ancestors from the Dark Continent. She comes to you direct from Paris . . . appearances before the crowned heads . . . main attraction at the Hippodrome . . . the subject of study by the greatest scientific minds of the century . . . etc.*

The legend was barefaced, bold. And no one had trouble believing she was genuine. Her eyes were flat, cloudy.

*

Well, here I am again. The poor man's Josephine Baker. Without the bananas and with an added panache. Or the poor man's Hottentot Venus — without the butt. I concentrate on keeping my eyes out of focus. If I do the people below me become indistinct. Just little patches of color, bright, dull. Sunday-best dims. As their shapes fade and soften, their noises seem to dim also. 'Oh!' 'Paris!' 'My God!' 'Wait your turn!' 'Indecent!' 'What a shame!' Better not mind what people say, or think.

You know, it's not easy being a freak; not even a pretend one — don't tell me you believed it for a minute. The Girl from Martinique was my idea. Yes indeed. In this business exotic is good, means a livelihood. I'm really the girl from Darktown. Left. One day just left. Took off to seek my fortune. Better to get fifty cents a day, room and board, for sitting here, white-washed and mysterious, than for lying on my back, or kneeling for that matter.

I live in a trailer with the Lobster Man. Nothing personal. We're the two coloreds in the show. Even freaks have their standards. But he's a nice man. No fake there. Born that way. Midwife had to twist and turn to get him out. Thought he would never walk but his mama prayed and rubbed and rubbed and prayed and slowly, slowly he began to move sideways. Can a nigger manage? I mean.

I mean he's down on all fours but he gets around. Well, you probably couldn't call it walking but he's under his own steam and that's good for something. He sleeps in a wooden box, he can fold himself up so small. Handy when you're sharing a trailer. I'm a big girl myself. Need all the room I can get. Never was enough room at home.

Last time I saw my mama was when I had to leave the show. Usual female reason — well, the Lobster Man said it didn't matter whose it was, we could raise it as ours. Thanks but no thanks — you know what I mean? So it was born back home and I left it — her — with my mama and that was the last time I was there. The place was still too small. My mama was glad of the new company, even though the baby sported evidence of *certain practices of her native land*. Dig? Mama's always been a race woman. I told her not to worry. Children darken as they grow. Lifting as they climb – Now girl, she interrupted me, don't you going being disrespectful. Oh, Mama, just take the little wood's colt and leave me in peace. You always wanted to start over with me. Here's your chance.

Yes, the Girl from Martinique was my idea but I didn't make her up. I read in a book that there was this little child back in slavery time – came out as a patchwork. So I got a couple of bottles of white shoe polish and – as La Bakaire would say – *voilà*! The child's name was Magdelaine. They put her on show as a baby. Called her *La Fille du Martinique*. I translated for the hometown crowd. Poor little thing. What a life!

There but for the grace of God, Agnes's father said, with no apparent logic.

She thought as she walked the village main street so many years from then, my God, I am more misshapen than they, stranger than she. Why think about that now? Other fairs had passed, other freaks. Why remember the Girl from Martinique?

Because she gave me nightmares?

Stove polish had probably achieved her effect, her father had reassured her, wondering why anyone white would ever want to be black, even partly so, even to make a living.

Isn't she real, Papa?

Only as real as any entertainment, Agnes.

Her father's hands.

Something stirred as she saw them, folded in front of him, as he calmly regarded the freaks. Gloved, at rest.

Agnes switched.

No, no, she must have started black. Must have. But

wasn't it against the law for a colored person to be white, even partly so? Even a patchwork?

Feeling sick at beholding her, Agnes was eager to stare. In the dark, under the tent, one hand moved, slid itself under her armpit and rested on her breast.

She had been given an unfortunate name. Her mother chose it, hoping her little lamb of God would feel the call, would be given the call by virtue of her name. But she had not. Had not felt the heat of vocation. Had not, but ought, she thought, to have been drawn to Him. She could have been saved, safe, with the Sisters of Mercy in Providence, rather than in the dangerous place her life had become.

But she did not feel the call, was at fault, and could not pretend – besides, she was damaged goods.

And then her father died, and her mother went legally blind from grief – the priest declared – and as the eldest daughter all choice was removed from her.

She should probably have pretended – to have spoken with the Blessed Virgin cloud-borne over the lake, ringed with stars, draped in her blue gown, roses blooming through the ice – blood-red and fragrant. Beseeching, commanding, begging Agnes to follow her. Forgiving. Or at least she could have conjured St Teresa, or Kateri Tekakwitha, the Lily of the Mohawks, whose sacred lake this had once been. But Agnes was afraid of Our Father's wrath should she pretend, and she had not the heart for devotion.

And no one would believe her – false or true.

The sisterhood had called her first cousin Cecelia, now Sister Augustine, splashing around in holy water, teaching math to city children. Fixing her coif looking into a spoon.

Agnes did as she was told. She stayed within the family's bosom; in fact became the bosom, upon which they rested their heads, wept, which her brother John clasped to him.

At the inquest – in her absence – the villagers said she had seemed happy. Always cheerful, content, no sign of anything.

Not an enemy in the world. She could be neither victim nor – what was the word used on TV? – perpetrator. Neither one. They thought further, paused. Just a little too eager for conversation. Yes. Wanted to know too much about other people's families, lives; asking, pressing them for details, past, business, children. She was hungry, it seemed. As if she had no family of her own. Wasn't there a son? someone asked. Didn't he die at birth? another wondered. No. No, that must have been someone else.

By and large she seemed happy – they concluded.

A woman held inside her a question Agnes had asked on the corner by the common just a few months before – Did your father ever teach you how to love a man?

None of the village had seen the Dalys – save Agnes – since the death of the father, and until the night of BOOM BOOM BOOM BOOM, as a bonfire raged by the church celebrating Independence, thinking at first the noise was fireworks, part of the festivities – some thought the rest of the Dalys had passed on and that Agnes had had them quietly buried on the farm.

Until the next morning, quite by chance, when they were laid bare for all to see, and pity, the Dalys kept to themselves – but for Agnes. The house in which she lived with her brother, son, sister, mother, was caught at the time of the father's death. A time of great need, loss, Depression. In the dark front room, entered by an unhinged door, screen torn and dusty, one wall was covered, decorated with pictures. Covers of LIFE – their window to the world. Black and white images – Hoover Dam, Shirley Temple, WPA Workers, Brenda Frazier – against a bright red logo. As the black and white images had become darker and fainter from the smoke of the woodfire, the red logo seemed to gain in brightness, so that if anyone entered the house, he or she was struck by LIFE LIFE LIFE LIFE emblazoned on the wall in front of them. But no one but the family was ever admitted, and that was part of the problem. Intercourse with outsiders took place through the scrim of the door, as if in a convent of Poor Clares.

Rita Hayworth's smoked-over face, kneeling in her lace negligée, head turned, gave credence to the church's explanation of the Black Madonna, held dear by the French-Canadians over the river.

The things women endured. God Almighty! Agnes had in her mind the story of a grandmother, told by an aunt some years before — at some family reunion, wedding or funeral or baptism, events her branch attended before their father's death, before they cut themselves off. The aunt threw back a tumbler of whiskey and proceeded to recite, as God is my witness that is what happened.

Her father, Agnes's grandfather, had stuffed a potato into his wife, her mother, Agnes's grandmother. This became family lore and a family joke because of the famine and all that entailed. Hardship.

Working on the railroad Agnes's grandfather was away a good deal of the time and needed to be clear in his mind. The job was dangerous, the foreman a bigot, the grandfather did not need the added concern. He'd seen men lose limbs.

So he took a spud — a small new potato, mind you — and stuffed it inside his wife. A potato from her own plot. The tale was told over whiskey and laughter and that was that.

Agnes did not know — or know to ask — what this did to her grandmother. Did she wrench the potato out, after seeing him safely off? Did she sleep with him ever after only under protest? Was she quietly relieved behind her widow's weeds when he fell from a trestle in the West and was returned to her in a square Railway Express box?

At school the other girls took out after Agnes and chastised her. It was as if she gave off a scent. They could not explain why she was chosen.

The nun in charge would occasionally swoop down on the

81

mob, scattering those in her path with threats and slaps, habit trapping some of the girls, but for the most part Sister let the girls blow off steam, their violence contained by the dirt floor and iron fence of a schoolyard.

Agnes had to stick up for herself, Sister reckoned. It was necessary, to get by in this life – unless, of course, the girl was to embrace martyrdom.

'Poor Agnes Violet Daly,' Sister told the Mother of her order, 'she is violated, is in agony daily.' Black habit trembling at this cleverness.

'Puberty often lends itself to frenzy,' the Mother put aside her *Boston Globe* to declare. 'There's always one.'

'Yes.'

'Have you spoken to Agnes yourself?'

'Mother?'

'I thought not.'

'Well, I did speak to her last week; rather, she spoke to me.'

'About?'

'She asked me if nuns were allowed into sideshows – '

'As exhibits?'

Sister smiled. 'I told her yes and she wanted to know if I had seen the sideshow at the tri-county fair this past summer.'

'And?'

'I said no and she walked away.'

'Curious child.'

The distance from the family farm to the parochial school was a long walk. A long walk but the only time Agnes had to herself, except those hours when she was asleep, and those were disturbed more and more, claimed by another.

On these walks, Agnes tried to come up with some strategy to counter the other girls, some clever words to defeat them, at least draw their attention away from her. But she found herself at a loss for words even when alone, and inevitably her search for words ended instead with images, full-color fantasies of a magnificent and startling fury. Walking the dirt road, kicking pebbles, Agnes's visions kept her company.

Some she gleaned from the *Tales of the Wild West* her grandfather left the family, others came from the *Lives of the Saints*, her grandmother's bequest. Agnes combed details from each anthology. These were the only real books in the house and they sparked Agnes's imagination; they held *true* stories.

Agnes buried girls to their necks in ant hills, smearing their faces with honey, sitting out of harm's way as the huge red ants took apart the mouth and eyes of a classmate. Girls screamed and wept their agony, turning to Agnes. She did not heed their pleas; in life, they did not hers.

Agnes led girls into an ambush of Redskins, flaming arrows arcing a blue sky, piercing the white sea-island-cotton breasts of the girls. Agnes stood back, to the side of the vision, as if invisible to the Redmen, watching and watching and doing nothing to save the sweet girlish bodies — unlike hers — against this pagan desecration. Accepting a flaming arrow from a fierce Apache, Agnes draws back the bow, lets loose, and watches as the fiery tip ignites the black of Sister's habit and she goes down in flames.

Girls spin on flaming wheels. Girls are impaled on iron spikes. Girls have their nipples torn off with red-hot pincers. Girls line the via Appia, nailed to crosses. And blessing this panorama, judging the punishment meet, was the Girl from Martinique, on her jungle throne, Queen of Heaven, intruder into Agnes's hagiography. Somehow she seemed right and Agnes let her be.

And in this company Agnes walks to school, and home again.

Her father told her King Solomon was the wisest and holiest of men and by right could have any virgin in his domain. Any one.

Agnes closed her eyes but the hagiography would not be summoned. Her father crashed against her imagination and she became part of his.

Her brother inherited her.

Her mother and sister said nothing.

Her brother was the father of her son.

Her mother told her to quit her job at the watch factory.

Her brother told her to keep the boy at home or else someone would find out.

She did.

She handed in her apron, brush and small container of radium.

BOOM BOOM BOOM BOOM. Jesus, Mary and Joseph, I should have done this years ago.

This 75-year-old odd quantity is flying through the dirt of the country in a Winnebago, on the run, heading for parts unknown. It is hot. She is alone.

The lake smokes behind her. The will-o'-the-wisp rising.

It was quite premeditated.

The week before, in the village, Agnes bought her ammunition. Barreling on in her jittery way to the man at the Mini-Mart about crows and scarecrows.

'I need to thin out the blackbirds. They're flying wild through the corn. Getting ready to devour it and it's nowhere near ready. The scarecrow's been stripped again. During the Depression hoboes would do that — for the clothes. Guess it's kids now . . . or maybe them vets. Hear about the one that was defrosted in the woods?' Agnes's voice slid into a cackle of a laugh, covered almost immediately by, 'Poor thing, poor thing. Must've been crazy.

'Happened last year too — stealing from the scarecrow. Had put one of my grandfather's old railroad vests on him . . . and my papa's doughboy hat. Don't know why the vets would want those old things . . . must be kids. Poor old scarecrow will be kindling soon enough . . . sad to see him standing there all naked in the field.

'Guess I'll just have to shoot the crows. So if anyone hears a noise you remember that . . . Then I'll string them on a clothesline and let the dead be a warning.'

She wondered if the man had even listened, and if he had, had she made sense? She'd never be able to do it in the light. And who went after crows in the pitch dark of a summer's night? Black on black. No full moon. Never mind. The man's head was down under the front counter where he kept the ammunition.

'One box do it?'

'Oh, mmm. I guess so. I can always come back for more.'

Funny. The hardest thing had been sliding the keys to the RV from her brother's pocket. Afraid he would sit upright and grab them from her – 'Now, Agnes, this doesn't concern you.'

But he was long gone.

His keys to the road, he had said. After a lifetime of working like a dog, and now that Mama is nearly dead, and summer people clamoring for the farm. Don't worry, we'll split it fair and square.

Well, not quite.

Inside the thing was nicely fitted out. Pots and pans and a TV set and linens and a CB radio and even a bathroom.

She was sad to leave the scrawny old scarecrow behind. All naked and miserable. Soon enough his limbs would freeze unless some kind soul cut him into kindling. Anything was better than being cold. Even burning.

After the blasts of the shotgun warmed her, Agnes prepared to leave the farm.

Before she started the Winnebago, before she slid into the seat and set off on her own, before she roared into the night, she lit the burning bush at the side of the porch. She wanted to light their way.

There was a soft whoosh as the gas ignited.

Screen Memory

T he sound of a jumprope came around in her head, softly, steadily marking time. Steadily slapping ground packed hard by the feet of girls.

Franklin's in the White House. Jump/Slap. *Talking to the ladies.* Jump/Slap. *Eleanor's in the outhouse.* Jump/Slap. *Eating chocolate babies.* Jump/Slap.

Noises of a long drawn-out summer's evening years ago. But painted in such rich tones she could touch it.

A line of girls wait their turn. Gathered skirts, sleeveless blouses, shorts, bright, flowered – peach, pink, aquamarine. She spies a tomboy in a striped polo shirt and cuffed blue jeans.

A girl slides from the middle of the line. The woman recognizes her previous self. The girl is dressed in a pale blue starched pinafore, stiff and white in places, bleached and starched almost to death. She edges away from the other girls; the rope, their song, which jars her and makes her sad. And this is inside her head.

She senses there is more to come. She rests her spine against a wineglass elm. No one seems to notice her absence.

The rope keeps up its slapping, the voices speed their chanting. As the chant speeds up, so does the rope. The tomboy rushes in, challenging the others to trip her, burn her legs where she has rolled her jeans. Excitement is at a pitch. Franklin! Ladies! Eleanor! Babies! The tomboy's feet pound the ground. They are out for her. A voice sings out, above the others, and a word, strange and harsh to the observer's ears, sounds over the pound of feet, over the slap of rope. *Bulldagger! Bulldagger! Bulldagger! Bulldagger!* The rope sings past the tomboy's ears. She feels its heat against her skin. She knows the word. Salt burns the corners of her eyes. The rope-turners dare, singing it closer and closer. Sting!

The girl in the pinafore hangs back. The girl in the pinafore who is bright-skinned, ladylike, whose veins are visible, as the ladies of the church have commented so many times, hangs back. The tomboy, who is darker, who could not pass the paper bag test, trips and stumbles out. Rubbing her leg where the rope has singed her. The word stops.

Where does she begin and the tomboy end?

Fireflies prepare to loft themselves. Mason jars with pricked lids are lined on the ground waiting to trap them. Boys swing their legs, scratched and bruised, from adventure or fury, from the first rung of a live oak tree. Oblivious to the girls, their singing — nemesis. The boys are swinging, talking, over the heads of the girls. Mostly of the War, their fathers, brothers, uncles, whoever represents them on air or land or sea.

The woman in the bed can barely make out their voices, though they speak inside her head.

Sudden lightning. A crack of thunder behind a hill. Wooden handles hit the dirt as the rope is dropped. Drops as big as an elephant's tears fall. The wind picks up the pace. Girls scatter to beat the band. Someone carefully coils the rope. Boys dare each other to stay in the tree.

The girl in the blue pinafore flies across the landscape. She flies into a window. To the feet of her grandmother.

Slow fade to black.

The woman in the bed wakes briefly, notes her pain, the dark outside.

Her head is splitting.

She and her grandmother have settled in a small town at the end of the line. At the edge of town where there are no sidewalks and houses are made from plain board, appearing ancient, beaten into smoothness, the two grow dahlias and peonies and azaleas. A rambling rose, pruned mercilessly by the grandmother, refuses to be restrained, climbing across the railings of the porch, masking the iron of the drainpipe, threatening to rampage across the roof and escape in a cloud of pink – she is wild. As wild as the girl's mother, whom the girl cannot remember, and the grandmother cannot forget.

The grandmother declares that roses are 'too showy' and therefore she dislikes them. (As if dahlias and peonies and azaleas in their cultivated brightness are not.) But the stubborn vine is not for her to kill – nothing, no living thing, is, and that is the first lesson – only to train.

While the rose may evoke her daughter, there is something else. She does not tell her granddaughter about the thing embedded in her thigh, souvenir of being chased into a bank of roses. Surely the thing must have worked its way out by now – or she would have gotten gangrene, lost her leg clear up to the hip, but she swears she can feel it. A small sharp thorn living inside her muscle. All because of a band of fools to whom she was nothing but a thing to chase.

The grandmother's prized possession sits against the wall in the front room, souvenir of a happier time; when her husband was alive and her daughter held promise. An upright piano, decorated in gilt, chosen by the King of Bohemia and the Knights of the Rosy Cross, so says it. The grandmother rubs the mahogany and ebony with lemon oil, cleans the ivory with rubbing alcohol, scrubbing hard, then takes a chamois to the entire instrument, slower now, soothing it after each fierce cleaning.

The ebony and the ivory and the mahogany come from Africa – the birthplace of civilization. That is another of the grandmother's lessons. From the forests of the Congo and the elephants of the Great Rift Valley, where fossils are there for the taking and you have but to pull a bone from the great stack to find the first woman or the first man.

The girl, under the eye of the grandmother, practices the piano each afternoon. The sharp ear of the grandmother catches missed notes, passages played too fast, articulation, passion lost sliding across the keys. The grandmother speaks to her of passion, of the right kind. 'Hastiness, carelessness, will never lead you to any real feeling, or,' she pauses, 'any lasting accomplishment. You have to go deep inside yourself – to the best part.' The black part, she thinks, for if anything can cloud your senses, it's that white blood. 'The best part,' she repeats to her granddaughter seated beside her on the piano bench, as she is atilt, favoring one hip.

The granddaughter, practicing the piano, remembers them leaving the last place, on the run, begging an old man and his son to transport the precious African thing – for to the grandmother the piano is African, civilized, the sum of its parts – on the back of a pick-up truck.

A flock of white ladies had descended on the grandmother, declaring she had no right to raise a white child and they would take the girl and place her with a 'decent' family. She explained that the girl was her granddaughter – sometimes it's like that. They did not hear. They took the girl by the hand, down the street, across the town, into the home of a man and a woman bereft of their only child by diphtheria. They led the girl into a pink room with roses rampant on the wall, a starched canopy hanging above the bed. They left her in the room and told her to remove her clothes, put on the robe they gave her, and take the bath they would draw for her. She did this.

Then, under cover of night, she let herself out the back door off the kitchen and made her way back, leaving the bed of a dead girl behind her. The sky pounded and the rain soaked her.

When the grandmother explained to the old man the circumstances of their leaving he agreed to help. To her granddaughter she said little except she hoped the piano would not be damaged in their flight.

There is a woman lying in a bed. She has flown through a

storm to the feet of her grandmother, who is seated atilt at the upright, on a bench which holds browned sheets of music. The girl's hair is glistening from the wet but not a strand is out of place. It is braided with care, tied with grosgrain. Her mind's eye brings the ribbon into closer focus; its elegant dullness, no cheap satin shine.

Fifty cents a yard at the general store on Main Street.

'And don't you go flinging it at me like that. I've lived too long for your rudeness. I don't think the good Lord put me on this earth to teach each generation of you politeness.' The grandmother is ramrod straight, black straw hat shiny, white gloves bright, hair restrained by a black net. The thing in her thigh throbs, as it always does in such situations, as it did in front of the white ladies, as it did on the back of the old man's truck.

The granddaughter chafes under the silence, scrutiny of the boy who is being addressed, a smirk creasing his face. She looks to the ceiling where a fan stirs up dust. She looks to the bolts of cotton behind his head. To her reflection in the glass-fronted cabinet. To the sunlight blaring through the huge windows in front, fading everything in sight; except the grandmother, who seems to become blacker with every word. And this is good. And the girl is frightened.

She looks anywhere but at the boy. She has heard their 'white nigger' hisses often enough, as if her skin, her hair signify only shame, a crime against nature.

The grandmother picks up the length of ribbon where it has fallen, holds the cloth against her spectacles, examining it, folding the ribbon inside her handkerchief.

The boy behind the counter is motionless, waiting for his father's money, waiting to wait on the other people watching him, as this old woman takes all the time in the world. Finally: 'Thank you, kindly,' she tells him, and counts fifty cents onto the marble surface, slowly, laying the copper in lines of ten; and the girl, in her imagination, desperate to be anywhere but here, sees lines of Cherokee in canoes skimming an icebound river, or walking to Oklahoma, stories her grandmother told her. 'They'd stopped listening to their Beloved Woman. Don't get me started, child.'

The transaction complete, they leave — leaving the boy, two dots of pink sparking each plump cheek, incongruous against his smirk.

The woman in the bed opens her eyes. It is still, dark. She looks to the window. A tall, pale girl flies in the window to the feet of her grandmother. Seated at the piano, she turns her head and the grandmother's spectacles catch the lightning.

'I want to stay here with you forever, Grandma.'

'I won't be here forever. You will have to make your own way.'

'Yes, ma'am.'

'We are born alone and we die alone and in the meanwhile we have to learn to live alone.'

'Yes, Grandma.'

'Good.'

They speak their set-piece like two shadow puppets against a white wall in a darkened room. They are shades, drawn behind the eye of a woman, full-grown, alive, in withdrawal.

'Did something happen tonight?'

'Nothing, Grandma; just the storm.'

'That's what made you take flight?'

'Yes, ma'am.'

'Are you sure?'

'Yes, ma'am.'

She could not tell her about the song, nor the word they had thrown at the other girl, to which the song was nothing.

She could not tell her about the pink room, the women examining her in the bath, her heart pounding as she escaped in a dead girl's clothes. They had burned hers.

94

Two childish flights. In each the grace which was rain, the fury which was storm chased her, saved her.

In the morning the sky was clear.

'Grandma?'

'Yes?'

'If I pay for it, can we get a radio?'

'Isn't a piano, aren't books enough for you?'

Silence.

'Where would you get that kind of money?'

'Mrs Baker has asked me to help her after school. She has a new baby.'

'Do I know this Mrs Baker?'

'She was a teacher at the school before we came here. She left to get married and have a baby.'

'Oh.' The grandmother paused. 'Then she is a colored woman?' As if she would even consider having her grand-daughter toil for the other ilk.

'Yes. And she has a college education.' Surely this detail would get the seal of approval, and with it the chance of the radio.

'What a fool.'

'Grandma?'

'I say what a foolish woman. To go through all that — all that she must have done, and her people too — to get a college education and become a teacher and then to throw it all away to become another breeder. What a shame!'

With the last she was not expressing sympathy for a life changed by fate, or circumstances beyond an individual's control; she meant *disgrace*, of the Eve-covering-her-nakedness sort.

'Yes, Grandma.' The girl could but assent.

The woman in the bed is watching as these shadows traverse the wall.

'Too many breeders, not enough readers. Yes — indeed.'

'She seems like a very nice woman.'

95

'And what, may I ask, does that count for? When there are children who depended on her? Why didn't she consider her responsibilities to her students, eh? Running off like that.'

Watching the shadows engage and disengage.

'She didn't run off, Grandma.'

No, Grandmother. Your daughter, my mother, ran off, or away. My mother who quit Spelman after one year because she didn't like the smell of her own hair burning – so you said. Am I to believe you? Went north and came back with me, and then ran off, away – again.

'You know what I mean. Selfish woman. Selfish and foolish. Lord have mercy, what a combination. The kind that do as they please and please no one but themselves.'

The grandmother turned away to regard the dirt street and the stubborn rose.

The granddaughter didn't dare offer that a selfish and foolish woman would not make much of a teacher. Nor that Miss Elliston – whose pointer seemed an extension of her right index finger, and whose blue rayon skirt bore an equator of chalk dust – was a more than permanent replacement. The bitterness went far too deep for mitigation, or comfort.

'Grandma, if I work for her, may I get a radio?'

'Tell me, why do you want this infernal thing?'

'Teacher says it's educational.' Escape. I want to know about the outside.

'Nonsense. Don't speak nonsense to me.'

'No, ma'am.'

'And just how much do you think this woman is willing to pay you?'

'I'm not sure.'

'What does her husband do, anyway?'

'He's in the navy; overseas.'

'Of course.' Her tone was resigned.

'Grandma?'

'Serving them coffee, cooking their meals, washing their

drawers. Just another servant in uniform, a house slave, for that is all the use the United States Navy has for the Negro man.'

She followed the War religiously, *Crisis* upon *Crisis*.

'Why didn't he sign up at Tuskeegee, eh? Instead of being a Pullman porter on the high seas, or worse.'

'I don't know,' her granddaughter admitted quietly, she who was half-them.

'Yellow in more ways than one, that's why. Playing it safe, following a family tradition. Cooking and cleaning and yassuh, yassuh, yassuh. They are yellow, am I right?'

'Yes, ma'am.'

'Well, those two deserve each other.'

It was no use. No use at all to mention Dorie Miller – about whom the grandmother had taught the granddaughter – seizing the guns on the *Arizona* and blasting the enemy from the sky. No use at all. She who was part-them felt on trembling ground.

Suddenly –

'As long as you realize who, what these people are, then you may work for the woman. But only until you have enough money for that blasted radio. Maybe Madame Foolish-Selfish can lend you some books. Unless,' her voice held an extraordinary coldness, 'she's sold them to buy diapers.'

'Yes, ma'am.'

'You will listen to the radio only at certain times, and you must promise me to abide by my choice of those times, and to exercise discretion.'

'I promise,' the girl said.

Poor Mrs Baker was in for one last volley. 'Maybe as you watch the woman deteriorate, you will decide her life will not be yours. Your brain is too good, child. And can be damaged by the likes of her, the trash of the radio.'

Not even when Mr Baker's ship was sunk in the Pacific and he was lost, did she relent. 'Far better to go down in flames than be sent to a watery grave. He died no hero's death, not he.'

> 'Full fathom five, thy father lies;
> Of his bones are coral made;
> Those are pearls that were his eyes:'

The baby with the black pearl eyes was folded into her chest as she spoke to him.

> 'Nothing of him that doth fade,
> But doth suffer a sea-change
> Into something rich and strange.'

She imagined a deep and enduring blackness. Salt stripping him to bone, coral grafting, encrusted with other sea-creatures. She thought suddenly it was the wrong ocean that had claimed him – his company was at the bottom of the other.

> 'Sea nymphs hourly ring his knell:
> Ding-dong.
> Hark! now I hear them – Ding-dong bell.'

She heard nothing. The silence would be as deep and enduring as the blackness.

The girl didn't dare tell the grandmother that she held Mrs Baker's hand when she got the news about her husband, brought her a glass of water, wiped her face. Lay beside her until she fell asleep. Gave the baby a sugar tit so his mother would not be waked.

The girl was learning about secrecy.

The girl tunes the radio in. Her head and the box are under a heavy crazy quilt, one of the last remnants of her mother; pieced like her mother's skin in the tent show where, as her grandmother said, 'she exhibits herself'. As a savage. A woman with wild hair. A freak.

That was a while ago; nothing has been heard from her since.

It is late. The grandmother is asleep on the back porch on a roll-away cot. Such is the heat she sleeps in the open air covered only by a thin muslin sheet.

The misery, heaviness of the quilt, smelling of her mother's handiwork, are more than compensated for by THE SHADOW. Who knows what evil lurks in the hearts of men?

The radio paid for, her visits to Mrs Baker are meant to stop – that was the agreement. But she will not quit. Her visits to Mrs Baker – like her hiding under her mother's covers with the radio late at night, terrified the hot tubes will catch the bed afire – are surreptitious, and fill her with a warmth she is sure is wrong. She loves this woman, who is soft, who drops the lace front of her camisole to feed her baby, who tunes in to the opera from New York on Saturday afternoons and explains each heated plot as she moves around the small neat house.

The girl sees the woman in her dreams.

On a hot afternoon in August Mrs Baker took her to a swimming hole a mile or two out in the country, beyond the town. They wrapped the baby and set him by the side of the water, 'Like the baby Moses,' Mrs Baker said. Birdsong was over them and the silver shadows of fish glanced off their legs.

'Come on, there's no one else around,' Mrs Baker told her, assuring her when she hesitated, 'There's nothing to be ashamed of.' And the girl slipped out of her clothes, folding them carefully on the grassy bank. Shamed nonetheless by her paleness.

Memory struck her like a water moccasin sliding through the muddy water. The women who would save her had her stand, turn around, open her legs – just to make sure.

She pulls herself up and comes to in her hospital bed. The piano in the corner of the room, the old lady, the girl, the jumprope, the white ladies, recede and fade from her sight. Now there is a stark white chest which holds bedclothes. In another corner a woman in a lace camisole, baby-blue ribbon threaded through the lace, smiles and waves and rises to the ceiling, where she slides into a crack in the plaster.

The woman in the bed reaches for the knob on the box beside her head and tunes it in; Ferrante and Teicher play the theme from *Exodus* on their twin pianos.

Her brain vibrates in a *contre coup*. She is in a brilliantly lit white room in Boston, Massachusetts. Outside is frozen solid. It is the dead of winter in the dead of night. She could use a drink.

What happened, happened quickly. The radio announced a contest. She told Mrs Baker about it. Mrs Baker convinced her to send her picture in to the contest: 'Do you really want to spend the rest of your days here? Especially now that your grandmother's passed on?' Her heart stopped. Just like that.

The picture was taken by Miss Velma Jackson, Mrs Baker's friend, who advertised herself as V. JACKSON, PORTRAIT PHOTOGRAPHY, US ARMY RET. Miss Jackson came to town a few years after the War was over, set up shop, and rented a room in Mrs Baker's small house. In her crisp khakis, with her deep brown skin, she contrasted well with the light-brown pasteled Mrs Baker. She also loved the opera and together they sang the duet from *Norma*.

When she moved in talk began. 'There must be something about that woman and uniforms,' the grandmother said in one of her final judgments.

Miss Jackson, who preferred 'Jack' to 'Velma', performed a vital service to the community, like the hairdresser and the undertaker. Poor people took care to keep a record of themselves, their kin. They needed Jack and so the talk died down. Died down until another photographer came along – a traveling man who decided to settle down.

Jack's portrait of the girl, now a young woman, came out

well. She stared back in her green-eyed, part-them glory against a plain white backdrop, no fussy ferns or winged armchairs. The picture was sent in to the contest, a wire returned, and she was summoned.

She took the plain name they offered her — eleven letters, to fit best on a marquee — and took off. A few papers were passed.

'Will you come with me?'

'No.'

'Why not?'

'I can't.'

'Why not?'

'Jack and I have made plans. She has some friends in Philadelphia. It will be easier for us there.'

'And Elijah?'

'Oh, we'll take him along, of course. Good schools there. And one of her friends has a boy his age.'

'I'm going to miss you.'

'You'll be fine. We'll keep in touch. This town isn't the world, you know.'

'No.'

Now there was nothing on the papers they sent — that is, no space for: *Race*?

Jack said: 'And what do you propose to do? Say, hey, Mr Producer, by the way, although I have half-moons on my fingernails, a-hem, a-hem?'

She was helped to her berth by a Pullman porter more green-eyed than she. In his silver-buttoned epauleted blue coat he reminded her of a medieval knight, on an iron horse, his chivalric code — RULES FOR PULLMAN PORTERS — stuck in his breast pocket. He serenaded her.

'De white gal ride in de parlor car.
De yaller gal try to do de same.
De black gal ride in de Jim Crow car.
But she get dar jes' de same.'

He looked at her as he stowed her bag. 'Remember that old song, Miss?'

'No.'

Daughter of the Mother Lode. The reader might recall that one. It's on late night TV and also on video by now. She was the half-breed daughter of a Forty-Niner. At first, dirty and monosyllabic, then taken up by a kindly rancher's wife, only to be kidnapped by some crazy Apaches.

Polysyllabic and clean and calicoed when the Apaches seize her, dirty and monosyllabic and buck-skinned when she breaks away – and violated, dear Lord, violated out of her head, for which the rancher wreaks considerable havoc on the Apaches. You may remember that she is baptized, and goes on to teach school in town and becomes a sort of mother-confessor to the dancehall girls.

As she gains speed, she ascends to become one of the more-stars-than-there-are-in-the-heavens, and her parts become lighter, brighter than before. Parts where 'gay' and 'grand' are staples of her dialogue. As in, 'Isn't she gay!' 'Isn't he grand!' She wears black velvet that droops at the neckline, a veiled pillbox, long white gloves.

She turns out the light next to the bed, shuts off the radio, looks out the window. Ice. Snow. Moon. The moon thin, with fat Venus beside it.

The door to the room suddenly whooshes open and a dark woman dressed in white approaches the bed.

'Mother?'

'Don't mind me, honey. I'm just here to clean up.'

'Oh.'

'I hope you feel better soon, honey. It takes time, you know.'

'Yes.'

The woman has dragged her mop and pail into the room and is now bent under the bed, so her voice is muffled beyond the whispers she speaks in — considerate of the drying-out process.

'Can I ask you something?' This soft-spoken question comes to the actress from underneath.

'Sure.'

'Would you sign a piece of paper for my daughter?'

'I'd be glad to.'

If I can remember my name.

The woman has emerged from under the bed and is standing next to her, looking down at her — bedpan in her right hand, disinfectant in her left.

The actress finds a piece of paper on the bedside table, asks the girl's name, signs 'with every good wish for your future'.

'Thank you kindly.'

She lies back. Behind her eyelids is a pond. Tables laden with food are in the background. In the scum of the pond are tadpoles, swimming spiders. Darning needles dart over the water's surface threatening to sew up the eyes of children.

A child is gulping pondwater.

Fried chicken, potato salad, coleslaw, pans of ice with pop bottles sweating from the cold against the heat.

The child has lost her footing.

A woman is turning the handle of an ice-cream bucket, a bushel basket of ripe peaches sits on the grass beside her. Three-legged races, sack races, races with an uncooked egg in a spoon, all the races known to man, form the landscape beyond the pond, the woman with the ice-cream bucket, the tables laden with food.

Finally — the child cries out.

People stop.

She is dragged from the water, filthy. She is pumped back to life. She throws up in the soft grass.

The woman wakes, the white of the pillow case is stained.

She pulls herself up in the bed.

The other children said she would turn green — from the

scum, the pondwater, the baby frogs they told her she had swallowed. No one will love you when you are green and ugly.

She gets up, goes to the bathroom, gets a towel to put over the pillow case.

'Hello. Information?'

'This is Philadelphia Information.'

'I would like the number of Velma Jackson, please.'

'One moment please.'

'I'll wait.'

'The number is . . .'

She hangs up. It's too late.

'She did run away from them, Mama. She came back to you. I don't think you ever gave her credit for that.'

'And look where she is now, Rebekah.'

'She ran away from them, left a room with pink roses. Sorry, Mama, I know how you hate roses.'

'Who is speaking, please?' The woman sits up again, looks around. Nothing.

What will become of her?

Let's see. This is February 1963.

She might find herself in Washington DC in August. A shrouded marcher in the heat, dark-glassed, high-heeled.

That is unlikely.

Go back? To what? This ain't *Pinky*.

Europe? A small place somewhere. Costa Brava or Paris – who cares? Do cameos for Fellini; worse come to worse, get a part in a spaghetti western.

She does her time. Fills a suitcase with her dietary needs: Milky Ways, cartons of Winston's, golden tequila, boards a plane at Idlewild.

Below the plane is a storm, a burst behind a cloud, streak lightning splits the sky, she rests her head against the window; she finds the cold comforting.

Election Day
1984

A woman stands on a snake of a line in the back of a born-again church in a coastal town in California. In places the line is slender, in others it bunches like a python after swallowing a calf, in a shot from *Wild Kingdom*. This is the polling place.

On the wall to the woman's right is a map, straight pins with colored heads indicating the positions of missionaries. She glances at the map, to see if any pins are fixed to her native land. Indeed. Her island so small that the huge blue head practically obliterates its outline.

On her left, through a glass, brightly, a Bible study class sits around a conference table on red plastic chairs, lips moving without a sound behind a window; all are women. She begins to hate them, fights it; whatever have they done to her? God.

She recites in her head: *Though I speak with the tongues of men and of angels and have not charity I am as a sounding brass or a tinkling cymbal.* If there is a hell (which she doesn't really believe but childhood is hard to shake) and if I am chosen to burn it will be because of this – which a teacher noted in the third grade, Palmer script flowing across the report card. *She holds herself aloof from the others.* There it was. Way back then.

'Where you from?' The woman in front of her, in a tan raincoat, a yellow fisherman's hat on her head, brown leather handbag strapped across her chest, turns suddenly to make conversation.

'New York.' She answers with the place she last was, not the place she is made of. Anyhow, she belongs there no longer. Her voice would not be recognized by her people. They are background.

'How long you been out here?'

'Two months.'

She is not being very friendly. The land is about to slide for Ronnie and surely this old lady is part of it, partly to blame, just as the parroting Bible class is. *Live and let live.* Her mother echoed in her head. *Slow to anger and abounding in steadfast love.* I hate their hate. *Two wrongs don't make a right. Judge not lest ye be judged.* Your father and I want for you and your brother a better life. There's no chance back there, that's all.

'How d'you get out here?'

'I drove.'

'Married?'

'No.'

'Alone?'

'Yes.'

'You weren't scared?'

'Not really.' *Liar.*

The line inches forward. People drip with unaccustomed rain. Every now and then someone says, 'But we need it.' And someone else nods.

'Isn't this country something?'

'Yes, it is.' She does not say beautiful, desolate.

'And where did you stop?'

The younger woman begins to recite her route. Her mind glosses her spoken words. Images flash like lantern slides. As if someone dropped the tray. Out of order.

'Detroit first. I visited friends.'

A rat sprints across the highway and a woman in a big Buick brakes – hard. Laughing with her friends in their backyard we brake for rats. The Heaven Hill is out of hand. She brakes hard, just like a woman. The totem pole – eagle on high – shadows them. Inside a turtle shell is sweetgrass. Indians inside cities raising corn. Totems. They turn to her, serious. Has she made the right decision? She strokes the sweetgrass, traces the quadrants of the turtle shell. Yes. I think so. The center fell out.

You're not running, are you? No. I don't think so. Sure?

Desert. In the distance a cluster of trailers. Wires crossing like spiders' webs. Smoke rises from thin pipes. Pick-ups. Children. Laundry supported on a slender thread. Everything slender, small, minute, at this distance. Nothing in the Rand-McNally. A cluster of people against red monuments, landscape laced with barbed wire. Dust cloud raised in the foreground as a roadrunner speeds by.

Labor Day Parade. Union floats. Reagan in an outhouse at the back of a UAW flatbed. A woman asks for a cigarette. 'Got a light too, sugar?' A dime? A dollar? A house? A home, honey?

'You got a place to put your head?'

'Yes.'

'You got kids?'

'No.'

'God bless, sister.'

River Rouge. Black Madonna. GOSPEL CHICKEN – OUR BIRD IS THE WORD! boarded up.

FREEDOM ROAD USED CARS: WE TOTE THE NOTE – rusts.

Mississippi. A plain green sign announces the King of the Waters. The Mici Sibi of the Chippewa. The final resting place of DeSoto. The river nobody wanted to be sold down. As wide as the Styx.

This is a country of waters and no water.

Glorious, ordinary the river runs.

Platte. Republican. Ohio. Little Blue. Des Moines.

In a backwater town of grain elevators and railway lines, roundhouses and old hotels, three women run a lunchroom. The wall behind the register is hung with their families. Beyond the lunchroom, the town, fields are a deep gold, pumps bow and rise, rhythm breaking the still of the landscape, in the distance a windbreak shelters a house.

She remembers from a history book in the eighth grade the photograph of a family, posed outside their sod house, amongst their valuables, chattel – Singer, piano, settee – brought into the light. *Moses Speese Family, Custer County, 1888.* That plain identification, with this opinion: *not all Negroes were downtrodden.*

FDR smiles from a wall in a lunchroom.

In the converted bank in Red Cloud hangs a letter from Langston Hughes to Willa Cather. Upstairs a diorama illustrates the Professor's room. Ántonia's cup and saucer are found behind glass. A few streets away is the perfect small white house. A small white house with an attic room where a girl plotted and planned to get away.

1961. Small apartment over a drugstore. World map over her bed. Jam jar with babysitting geld. Lying there in the heat of a summer night, regarding France, her goal back then, the woman above them playing over and over, 'I always knew I'd find someone like you, so welcome to my little corner of the world.' Husband shouting to shut the goddamned phonograph off. The woman chanting. 'Hit me, hit me, go ahead and hit me.' Quiet then.

Farmland turns high plains.

A stone is fixed to the ground. ON THIS SPOT CRAZY HORSE OGALLALA CHIEF WAS KILLED SEPT 5, 1877. This one will stand for the others.

She sends a postcard of the marker to her brother.

Dear Bill,
I'm okay. Thought you'd like (stupid word) to have this. Visited Cather's house and museum in Red Cloud. Lots of stuff. But no red carnation. Was it a *red* carnation?

Love, Jess

Salt Lake. A city set in yellow. In the tabernacle, imposing, a family, intact, divine, walks on air.

At a gas station a man throws her change at her and calls her a wetback. What tipped him off? Her speech is plain. Her skin has a tinge but could deceive the untutored eye. Her hair curls at the edges. But permanents are 'in'. Perhaps not in Salt Lake. She almost laughs but realizes the danger. She revs the Mustang and lets the silver rattle on the floor.

She fought the desire to call out *Adios!* Spanish is her third language.

A tired waitress in an all-night diner serves her eggs and coffee, her skin sallow from the atmosphere. 'You're not from around here, are you?'

'No.'

The great white lake lies on either side of her. Black highway a thin ribbon between water and salt. Light refracting color here and there.

She turns on the tape deck and Bob Marley sings about loss and future and past and, no, woman, no cry. And she does. Her tears run salt into her mouth.

She crosses into Nevada. Stops at a restaurant on a bright Sunday morning and feeds a machine until she feels refreshed. An old man with a cup of quarters wedged in his belt feeds the one beside her. As she turns to leave, a woman in a cowboy hat, wild bird feather garnishing its rim, storms in, pushing the old man from his spinning cherries, bells, oranges. 'Jesus Christ! A person can't even go get something to eat!'

'Don't mind her,' the old man says, 'she's just protecting her investment.'

In her silver Motown prairie schooner, packed with books and all else she owns, she is driving west. She crosses into California at the Donner Pass, observes the monument to the pioneer spirit, and heads down the Sierra to the Pacific.

*

'My last stop before here was Reno.'

'When you passed through Nebraska, did you drive through Omaha?'

'Yes. Is that where you're from?'

'No. I'm native Californian. From Bakersfield. But I was in Omaha once. In and out.'

'Oh.'

'Did you visit Boys' Town when you passed through?'

The old woman asks this matter-of-factly, as if an orphanage was one of the top ten tourist attractions. Right beside Disneyland, Mount Rushmore, Wounded Knee.

'No.'

'That's too bad. It's a wonderful place. At least it was when I was there. Nineteen thirty-five. Of course, everything changes. That Father Flanagan was a saint. But you're probably too young to remember him.'

The younger woman nods politely. She sees only Spencer Tracy, in black and white, on a nineteen-inch screen, getting tough with Mickey Rooney.

'I took a boy there once.'

The old woman declares this quietly, dropping her voice, moving closer, beckoning the stranger closer, at once transforming the dialogue.

The younger woman is startled. Brother? Cousin? Nephew? Son? Who? She doesn't dare ask. She thinks she has met an ancient mariner, one who walks the coast, telling.

'Really?'

'Yes. Really. Like I said, it was nineteen thirty-five. The depth of the Depression. Just took him and drove from Bakersfield to Omaha. Almost nonstop. Didn't take that long, you know. Most of the traffic was going in the other direction.' She smiles.

The child slept in the back for most of the journey. Covered with a plaid blanket. He twitched in his sleep, whimpered now and then. The desert. Her black car eating up the rays. The child remained wrapped in the blanket, suffering from a coldness, seeming not to notice the heat, light, LAST CHANCE FOR GAS BEFORE wherever. She was washed in sweat.

She sang to pass the time, to keep them – herself – company. The desert past, they cross the Sierra. Oh, mine eyes have seen the glory of the coming of the Lord/ He is trampling out the vintage where the grapes of wrath are stored. It is written in her will that they will sing it at her graveside.

She tried to get the boy to join her, but he hadn't the heart to sing. Else he didn't know the words, but she did try to teach him. The boy was too shy, frightened, to ask for food, for a drink of water, to use the bathroom. So she stopped when she thought it might be necessary and that seemed to work. It was a spinster's best solution – what did she know about children?

She stopped the car for a rest. Poured a canvas bag of water into the desperate radiator. Sitting on the running board while the car drank, sitting there they watched the people from the Dust Bowl pass them by. Each traveling band had a song. California, here I come.

People sang back then. Sang themselves through all kinds of things.

'Just you and the boy?'

'Yes.' Yes, me and the boy and I didn't even know his name. Finally got it out of him in Colorado. He didn't know the year of his birth, so I made one up.

'Yes. Just the two of us. We were in a big hurry, you see, so they picked me. I had the most reliable car, for one thing. And there wasn't any reason for anyone else to come along.'

'Who was "they"?'

'A group of women from my church. Baptist. Anyway, my car was pretty good, four new tires, and I was unattached and could get away at a moment's notice, and there wasn't anyone to miss me. Being a single woman and all. I just put a sign on the door. Closed due to illness. I ran a small grocery store. Inherited it from my father. The kind of place you hardly ever see nowadays.'

'What happened?'

'Well, we got to Omaha and I turned the boy over to Father Flanagan.'

'I mean what happened before? Why? Why did you have to take him there? Didn't anyone want him?'

She, the child-immigrant, knows intimately the removal of children. She takes the boy's part, her suspicion drenched in assumption. 'Didn't you want him?'

'Wasn't mine to want, dear. Listen, it's a long story, but I've come this far. And this line is moving awfully slow – and not much at the end of it.' She smiled again and the younger woman couldn't help but join her.

'He was ten years old about. He lived with his mother and father on a small ranch at the edge of town – they were tenants, not owners – poor people. Once, when one of the church women visited the ranch with a basket for the family – which is what we need to be doing now, especially with Thanksgiving just around the corner; you can't just do it holiday time, though. Well, anyway, this was in the summer, and the church woman called on the family. She noticed, couldn't help *but* notice, that the woman who answered the door, the boy's mother, was bruised, all purple and yellow, on her face, hands, neck – everywhere not covered by her clothes. So the visitor gave the woman the basket and asked her who had beaten her – not right out, mind you, but as clear as she could make the question. And of course the woman said no one. What else could she say? The visitor told the woman that if things got so bad she couldn't stand it, she should call the minister's wife and talk to her and the minister would come and talk to the woman's husband.

'Well, the woman explained to the visitor that they had no telephone, but the visitor persisted, so the woman said, okay, if things got too bad she'd call from the pay phone at the filling station down the road. I don't think she ever intended to call on her own account. I mean, getting a minister, a stranger . . . it wasn't the brightest suggestion . . . probably would have only made things worse for her . . . anyway, the visitor left and the woman nodded and thanked her for the basket and that was that.

'Then one night the minister's wife took a call, and the voice at the other end was expressing itself in these fierce whispers. The voice was very upset, but the woman was taking care not to be overheard. Finally, the minister's wife put two and two together; she called me and I called a couple of other women – we were the ladies' auxiliary of the church, you see. Well, we got in my car and went out to the ranch.'

She paused for breath and looked around, but no one else was listening.

Her voice slowed, each syllable carefully pronounced. 'It was the damnedest sight I ever saw, or ever hope to see. Not even as a Red Cross girl, in the war, in New Guinea.

'The ranch house had a dutch door – remember those? – the kind where the top is separate from the bottom?'

The younger woman nodded. Fifties TV. A woman dressed in a frilly apron calls the boys in for brownies.

'Well, the top half was swinging wide open. On the porch, outside the door, was this man, lying on his back, his face just gone. Blowed off. Nothing.

'Inside, you could see this little boy sitting on some steps, holding a shotgun, crying and wiping his nose on his sleeve. His mother was sitting next to him, face as blank as they come. Ugly red line under her chin.

'We decided then and there to get him out of town. I mean, he had his whole life ahead of him. Why should he be punished? It was an easy choice, believe me.

'It was much harder convincing these Baptists that Father Flanagan's place would be the place to take the boy. But *we* were the Baptists, Lord knows what the boy and his people were. Better there than a reform school. I told them about an article I had read in the *Saturday Evening Post* and all about

Father Flanagan and him saying "there is no such thing as a bad boy" and so on, and it was decided. And we didn't even think to call the men in on this, that was for later.

'We packed up and left that very night. We told the mother it was for the boy's own good and she seemed to agree, though she didn't say much. Shock.'

'Did *he* say anything?'

'Hardly a word between there and Omaha. Not even when we reached the freedom road – you know, where the Mormons are supposed to have planted sunflowers along the way? I wanted to tell him what I knew, tried too, to tell him it wasn't the Mormons, it was the Indians – his people, you see.'

'You didn't say they were Indians.'

'Well, I think they were. They never said for sure. But I think it was a safe guess. They looked like it. Even if he wasn't, it was a nice story I told him: how they weren't just flowers, but holding the flower to the ground was something like a potato. Food the Indians planted during the wars on the plains. But I don't know how much got through to him, all wrapped up in the back.'

'Couldn't you have found out from his mother where their people were?'

The old woman sighed. 'I was trying to do what I thought was best. There wasn't time and, well, the woman wasn't talking. Indians can be difficult, but coming from New York you wouldn't know that.'

The younger woman says nothing.

'I tried to tell him that if someone bullies and beats up on people they have to expect what they get – shouldn't expect no better. And he was only trying to come between his mother and another beating – or worse. Are you listening?'

'Pardon?'

'I didn't think so . . . Look, better Boys' Town than some God-forsaken reservation . . . where he would drown in whiskey or die from TB.'

'I understand what you are saying. But . . .'

'His mother wouldn't talk. He wouldn't talk – even if he knew who his people were. Even if all the Indians had mailing addresses and I had all the time in the world . . . I don't know. Maybe his mother didn't talk because she thought I was doing what was best for him.'

The younger woman withdraws further into silence, waiting now only for the end of the story, the end of the line.

'I don't know how much he understood of what I told him. Most of the time he seemed to be sleeping. Or I could hear him crying. Most of the time I talked – or sang. What a pair, eh?'

She will not relinquish her reminiscence, the flavor of it, the goodness of it. And what did you get out of it? Adventure? Righteousness?

The younger woman thinks she sees the boy clearly. The tracks of children running from the Christian boarding schools, feet frozen in the snow. She's not a historian for nothing.

She asks the inevitable question: 'Whatever happened to him?'

'I don't know. I never saw him after I left him at Boys' Town. But the police never found out where he was, either. That was good. I mean, that was the point of the whole journey. A safe place.'

'What about . . . ?' The younger woman is caught up again.

'The mother? She wasn't so lucky. She went to prison for life. Manslaughter.'

'Didn't she try to get away? I mean why didn't she run?'

'And where would she go? A woman like that – traveling alone?'

'Maybe she was heartbroken.'

They reached the voting booths, having traveled the last few yards in silence.

Bodies of
Water

An old woman is sitting in the middle of an icebound lake. She has a basket and a Thermos and is herself wrapped in layers of wool and down. She is seated on a camp stool. Her lips move.

She is singing to bring in the fish, she would say, should you ask her, gather them into the round opening at her feet, cut with the saw now wrapped in a flannel rag set beside her on the ice. She has spent a lifetime cutting. Ice. Wood. Stone. Her maul handled anew many times by now, her wedge gray steel, no trace of the manufacturer's gay blue paint.

As she sings, mist escapes her mouth. She is cold. What fish? Trout; maybe perch. At this time of year? *I want something small.* She needs to feed no one beside herself, and has no heart for freezing.

The cold drove them to the deepest, cleanest part of the lake. Would her sound reach them as they slept? Would anyone underwater hear the singer? Or is her voice lost? *Sweet Molly Malone* caught in the winter light.

The gray of the afternoon rests on the old woman's shoulders and she sips her whiskey-laced tea between snatches of song.

Truth be told, she sings to keep herself awake. No fish come. She is fighting sleep.

In a stone cottage at the water's edge a younger woman watches the old woman.

The house is new to her: hers, not-hers. Frozen into the silence of the season, where no birds sing. White flakes glance against the window frosted from the cold and heat cast by the woodstove. She draws her hand across the pane and watches. The old woman.

The lake. Enclosed, deep, cold. A cold which could stop time — she likes to think. The best lakes were hidden, safe, glacial. She is drawn to lakes, yet afraid of water.

She could see with her mind's eye her girlhood — one day, one afternoon. Her rising womanly from the waters. At twelve, or thirteen. The water laps at her and the black snakes of a mountain lake whisper past her. A tangle of hair reaches past her shoulders. The smell of freshwater is around her. Hard black waterbugs play around her legs. That is the picture in her mind. Standing in the shallows, moving forward, the Lady of Legend emerges from her element. And that image is joined in memory to another — lying belly-down on her single bed, the soft reds and muted blues of NC Wyeth in a storybook. She couldn't read yet; her brother could. It was his book, won in a city-wide reading competition. The Lady's upraised hand, the sword.

'Your brother reads too much.'

That summer at that mountain lake he had not been with them. Sent to some tough place, while she had the parents to herself. Two weeks in a rented cabin. The smell of knotty pine overwhelming. Counting the knots, trying to bring on sleep.

Six cabins circled a towering pole, Stars and Stripes flapping over families, brought down each evening by the owner's Boy Scout son. He set the flag at half-mast the summer Marilyn Monroe died; his mother thought that was disrespectful and yanked the banner to full height, warning her boy not to be so smart.

The younger woman sees herself rising from the waters of that mountain lake. In the frozen glass beyond which an old woman sits on the ice.

Her father's laughter as he saluted his little mermaid.

Her mother: 'Mind! Snakes!' And the girl ran out of the water, convinced a snake had wrapped around her legs; a waterbug made its way into the tangle of her sweet new hair — of which her parents were ignorant — and in that instant, giving way to her mother's warning, the delicacy of her relationship with snakes, bugs, water, weeds, had been violated, changed. That simple.

The younger woman is warm in the cottage. She feels hidden, safe. In thick wool socks and plaid Pendleton, soft brown corduroys wrapped around her legs.

In the foreground a cardinal is poking through drifts. His flash of color the only color of the afternoon. He captures her attention, draws her from herself, the old woman. Tomorrow she will venture forth, walk to the village to buy birdseed. There is a wooden feeder, handmade, hanging from a bare catalpa. In that tough place they taught her brother carpentry.

The old woman had thought it too cold for snow, but flakes are swirling around her. The wind is coming down hard from the hills and sweeping across the lake, no break in sight. No break but a few tall pines – *scorned as timber, belovéd of the sky*. She remembers another old woman's words; one who lived alone in the wild and painted totems.

She sniffs at the snow and sticks out her tongue to catch a few flakes, rocking her head from side to side. Too much whiskey, old girl, she tells herself.

'Or are you entering your second childhood?'

She recalls the familiar taunt of a niece, her dead brother's elder daughter, who takes it upon herself to keep family members in line. Not a dreadful woman, merely unimaginative, and terrified of any imaginative act. Little things set her off. Once the old woman sent the niece's daughter a book about the witch trials at Salem. The niece responded as if the old woman was a purveyor of magic.

Poor soul. But dangerous too.

She would sometimes follow the taunt with a definite threat, one determined to get the old woman's attention.

'For if you are, we shall have to make arrangements.'

Yes, *arrangements*. For what? A nursery? Padded cell? A

bit of both. A room (shared with a stranger, strangers) where she would be spoon-fed – everything mashed beyond texture or recognition. Probably tied to her bed by night, her chair by day. Where the stench of urine would be as unrelenting as a bank of lilac in bloom. Where she – who had chosen childlessness, another of the niece's peeves – would be perpetually asked: Where are your children? Grandchildren?

She had seen these places for herself. She had seen enough friends locked away in places where a sign on the door warned visitors: DON'T LEAVE KEYS IN CAR. As if a horde of old women (for the inmates of these homes were mostly women) would seize the day, the chance to escape, and take the curves of the Mohawk Trail at unsafe speeds, endangering innocent bystanders.

At first the sign made her smile, but nothing about this was funny.

The physical restraints, the lack of movement, were not the worst of it. She had seen women shrivel before her eyes, with nothing to occupy their minds but the pettiness of people in a confined space, where one group had total control over the other. Where the library consisted of *Reader's Digest* condensed books, the Bible, out-of-date magazines. And, as unrelenting as the stench, the noise of the television.

The niece had erupted most recently when another old woman died, and her aunt was named – for all the world to read – in the weeklies and dailies of the valley as 'sole survivor'.

'Jesus, I've always suspected as much, but why did she have to advertise it?'

'You worry too much,' her husband tried to calm her. 'Any reasonable person will see it for what it is.'

'Which is?'

'Two old maids. That's all.'

The niece forwarded the old woman yet another brochure, enclosing a note. 'This seems a pleasant place – now that your "friend" is gone.'

Not if she could help it. No. She had her own money stashed where they couldn't find it. If need be she would take off, head West, change her name. She had her escape hatch. They wouldn't take her alive.

She thought about crazy old Agnes, disappearing without a trace while the village gathered to salute the Bicentennial, erasing her family in cold blood.

Now, *that* was wrong.

The escape?

The murders.

She is murmuring to herself.

Really? Even after what they found out?

No. That sort of thing is always wrong. There are certain absolutes.

They had gone to school together. She could see Agnes, off somewhere, cowed by the other girls, and her other life – the one lived away from the nuns. A strong girl, red hair, green eyes, Irish to the T. Never able to give as good as she got. She was outnumbered.

And she, old woman now, girl then, had done not a thing to lessen the odds.

That was wrong.

Did I know it then?

Get up, old girl, before they send the wagon for you.

Now – to home. Stir the fire. Choose a volume for the evening. See if the old black and white stray is around, as hoary and as sweet as the older Whitman. As she imagines the older Whitman. She will invite him in – never does he accept. She speaks softly to him on the porch, in the dark, his eyes like hard glass reflectors. He will take the pork chop bone, the remains of the baked potato, the dish of warmed milk – but not the shelter. Each time she makes the invitation, then leaves him to eat in peace.

She longs for warmth suddenly and wishes she could float to the clapboard house far older than she is.

Her head sinks forward and she knows she will either

sleep there and freeze, or make her way home. She rises, carefully, her breasts have sunk into her belly; she lifts them.

She pours the remains of her Thermos onto the ice, as libation for the spirits, the manifestations. Next time they may guide the fish to her, if they are not too busy with better things. Tea dances. Bridge. Gossip. However they occupy themselves in their watery parlors.

She pictures them not draped in gossamer, but bugle-beaded, ghosts who dangle chainmail evening bags from their thin wrists. These ladies of the lake.

Do they make their own music?

And how do they get on with the others? All draped in bombazine, the heavy black of mourning clothes.

Widows and glamour girls – together forever.

And the others?

How many souls collide underwater?

Enough.

She folds the camp stool and gathers her creel and rod and reel, snapping the rod into a walking stick. Her gear is slung over one shoulder and she moves forward on the ice.

The younger woman watches still. Watches as the old woman makes a false step and slips. Starts, and wonders if she should run across the lake. Immediately the old woman has risen again, and is off again – strongly. The younger one relaxes, sipping her coffee, turning back to the desk.

Raising her head as a snow-cloud crosses the lake, the younger woman fancies a shape, not able to make it out, the wind swirls so.

II

The old woman retreated in winter to one room at the back of the eight-chambered house. Built on and on on one level, from parlor to bedroom, to kitchen, to birthing room, to mud kitchen to breezeway to woodshed. The peaked roof

126

gave the house the illusion of two stories, but held only a crawl space, the habitat of bats.

One room was hers, which she wrapped around her, and cushioned with all manner of souvenir, which she sometimes regards as comfort, sometimes as detritus. Recently she has needed her stuff more than before. That's natural, she thinks, sometimes.

A horsehair sofa stands in one corner opposite the fire – unto itself. Severe – as it had been when it stood in the waiting room of her father's office.

A child sitting in this waiting room, on this high-backed sofa, legs crossed at the ankles, as her father taught her, waiting, reading; always reading. Hour upon hour waiting, while her father searched deeds, negotiated rights of way, delayed liens. Property, the ownership and distribution thereof, had been his specialty. A man of substance, but not without compassion. The less fortunate, as she had been taught to call them, came to him. Flocked. The men and women and children who perched on the edge of this selfsame sofa, lacking the surety to sit back, leaving no mark on the hard black hide. Unlike some others – there was a scar on the armrest where the monsignor, visiting from Holy Cross, had set his cigar.

She sat reading, always reading, unless one of her father's clients, or two, or three, spoke to her. Politeness was valued: a child did not withdraw when addressed by an adult, no matter who, no matter how fascinating her book, how urgent her inner life. People she knew only by sight asked after her school, her brothers, her aunts and uncles, and, finally, her father, carefully avoiding the subject of *mother*, since the girl's birth had been the occasion of the woman's passing. Poor child, she needs a woman's touch, they said to each other in one breath, in another slightly resenting this girl who had made her father a lonely man.

They would talk and she would respond, lower her eyes, smile, nod, whatever the litany called for. But she was uncomfortable with them, and forced herself not to withdraw when they addressed her, and did as they demanded. In between their words, their eyes were fixed on the wavy glass window, bathroom glass, distorting the shapes inside the inner office – what her father called his *sanctum sanctorum* – the gilt lettering stating, EDWARD DILLON ATTORNEY-AT-LAW. The brass knob turning from time to time and a tall dark man, Black-Irish, as handsome as the devil, calling 'Next'.

She sleeps on this sofa in winter, her heavy contours denting its surface, her scent entering it. The black leather cracked in a few places, but the piece, the structure, intact. They don't make things the way they used to. That's a fact.

At night she spreads a white muslin sheet, places pillows at one end, and covers herself with a quilt pieced by another woman, for which she herself cut the template.

Wrapped in these bits and pieces, a stack of books on the floor beside her, she allows her mind to wander. Now, even with *The Years* propped on her chest, her mind strays – she lets it – eyes lighting on a patch, determining its beginning, as sundress, robe, silk blouse with jabot, boastful intricate stitches fixing each piece to the other – she is gone somewhere beyond the book. Back.

Bessie taught her about quilts. They spoke of cartography, biography, history, resistance. Drunkard's Path. Road to California. Underground Railroad. Mohawk Trail. Bessie taught her about patterns, taught her how to cut, let her watch as she threaded the needle, leading steel and thread through cloth, stopping to consider direction, contrast, harmony, shade, color.

Theirs was a friendship begun in girlhood. Picking strawberries in thin cotton. Hands stained where the red tenderness gives way, thin cotton sticking to their upper legs. The redness of them, from berries, the August sun. They were in an old peach orchard near the lake. Someone else's land – abandoned. Gorged on berries they attack the peaches, the heavy fuzz of the fruit against their mouths. Their skin itches from the fuzz and they fly to the edge of the water and plunge in fully dressed.

'Ever been really kissed?' Who had been so daring as to ask that? In their wet dresses, sun sparkling the water on their red cheeks, two pink tongues met, and the two held fast.

On this cold night the snow flies around a mailbox at the side of the road. ANNE DILLON. ISABELLA STRANIERE.

She has not had the heart to remove the other name.

She could barely tell the bees.

III

January something,
the year of the piano

Dear Jess,
Hope you are able to find everything. The cupboard next to the fridge is well-stocked and should hold you until you begin to find your way around. Nothing fancy. For essentials you can try the Mini-Mart at the edge of the village. Otherwise you'll need to 'go to town'.

Booze is underneath the breakfront by the dining table. Coffee beans in the freezer. Seasoned wood in the box just inside the back door – extra in the shed out back.

Défense de fumer. At least, I hope you've abandoned that particular death-defying habit. Listen to me. Hah! One good thing about all this, I won't have to quit after all. I can turn my fingertips burnt sienna if I please.

I've told the postmaster that I am going away and that you are using the place while I'm gone. No need to be specific. As long as they have some sense of what's happening with people's places, they're content. Curious but not nosy. Great happiness – but not now. Remember?

(She did. Her Greek landlady in London when she was in full flight, who read her coffee grounds and intoned the same prophecy each time. With henna hair and black eyes, in perpetual mourning for her White Russian husband and the baby she aborted in a bathtub.)

Don't know what they'd think if they knew but probably no different than urban types.

Don't worry. Even if your ears ring when they hold town meeting. Smile.

God loves you. Smile.

Seriously, I hope you stay well and that the place gives you what you need. At least something of what you need. It's been too long not seeing each other, but you'll glimpse me here. More than glimpse. And, let's face it, we're very different people, and probably would be at each other's throats before long.

(She lit a cigarette, inhaling deeply. Watching the ember flare, then fall. Turning to watch the roads of fire in the stove. The smoke only made the eye-water worse.)

It will be frozen and cold for weeks to come but the spring will be worth it all. Watch for false hellebore — it has greenish-white flowers and grows on the floor of the pine forest beyond the lake. After the skunk cabbage they are about the next sign to appear. Then you will see trillium, pink and white, rampant green. You will know it's truly spring when you see a ladyslipper. They're warm pink and lavender, like a wild orchid. O'Keeffe could never do them justice, the sensuality of them.

Probably no one could.

I don't think I will ever just see the ladyslipper, the pine, the sun dropping without, you know, thinking O'Keeffe, Carr, Friedrich, or another trio. I have never been able to behold nature alone. But then you know that. Behold — funny word. I think it has to do with the need for human description, definition. Unless we describe it, oh, I don't know.

Don't you find O'Keeffe's work unbearably cold? I do. Cold old bitch of the desert. Our Lady of the Obvious. Sorry. Sorry. Sorry. *Mea Culpa. Mea Maxima Culpa*, aka Maxine Culpa, the famous nun cum scat-singer.

Rude boy!

Sorry, my love, I am meandering. Pray that this thing doesn't get me in the head, will you? I think I could take anything but that. This old head has already been through a lot. But do you know when it's that, or are you so far gone . . . no . . . God . . . I didn't mean to lay that out here. Of course it must be a matter of degree. A slice of bread going slowly stale, finally the soft spot at the center hardens – that's it.

To this day jelly sandwiches make me puke. And they said I wouldn't remember.

Last spring I found a beaver lodge at the far end of the lake. You could hear the babies.

I hear that in the city there's a run on all the channeling books, mediums (media?), whatever. Well, I think I'll get me a ouija board and call up Winslow Homer. Silly old queen. What makes people think the dead have time for the living? Or that someone you wouldn't be caught dead with in life deserves a hearing? Pathetic, isn't it? God, listen to me.

Why don't people channel Carole Lombard – I ask you that. Instead of all these drunks, bores, extraterrestrials?

Because Shirley MacLaine isn't a faggot, that's why. You heard it here first.

Poor old Carole Lombard, the last thing she needs is fans nagging her in the Great Beyond.

I should be burned at the stake, like Joan of ARC. Burned at the stake, scattered on the quenelles of Rouen, fed to the mayor, and my heart put in a box above the altar. My relic. Now where did all *that* come from?

(She got up and walked over to the stove, playing a poker through the coals. Choosing a thin log of birch she watched the bark catch and curl.

131

She wrote him a letter on birchbark, pretending she was an Indian. Crazy Horse was his hero when they were kids.)

Characters. Not to change the subject, but . . . yes, there are plenty of characters. You will no doubt see Miss Dillon fishing on the lake. As I write this I can see her, all wrapped up and sitting on her camp stool. She doesn't seem to catch anything — mostly I think it's a form of meditation. I know her by sight and from things overheard at the PO. I think I've been here too long. Over-concern with country matters.

Anyhow, if you see an old woman on the lake — and you will — that's who she is. I gather her lifelong friend passed on (Jesus! Why can't I just say died?) a while ago. The friend (and why, for God's sake, can't I say lover? — the old girl *was* listed in the obits as 'sole survivor') was a schoolteacher, Miss Straniere. The 'sole survivor' thing caused a little bit of talk. The postmistress stopped one group cold with, 'Well, I reckon that's what she is.'

You know and I know why I can't say 'died'. So much easier to think of passing, floating, dancing on a fucking moonbeam. It's like waiting for a fucking car crash . . . head on . . . but very, very messy (say that like Bette Davis, please) and in slow, slow motion. As for 'lover', my prejudice, I guess.

Miss Dillon kept the house and garden, sold maple syrup and watercolors to the summer people. (Mostly scenes of the lake, some quite surreal. Lots of mist and foxfire. Skeletal trees at the borders. Perhaps you'll get to see them; the Mini-Mart exhibits them during the season.) I know that sounds like Patience and Sarah on Golden Pond or something. She must be very lonely. No, that's presumptuous.

I am the one that's lonely.

This is the fifth draft of this letter. I *am* trying not to be morbid. Bear with me.

Try to enjoy yourself.

When you go to town — as opposed to village — to shop,

you might want to check out the Atheneum. Wonderful woodwork inside and an actual Bierstadt. El Capitan. How he lit those huge landscapes.

Here I am again. You go to El Capitan (although I'm glad California did not claim you), probably sleep outside or something. I look at the Bierstadt three thousand miles away and have seen it.

After the thaw, you never know what might show up. Last spring a bunch of kids found a guy who had run away from the VA hospital. Poor bastard. Propped against a wall in a wrecked old farmhouse in the woods. Fell asleep in the cold. Yesterday's news on his head.

After the thaw and once the frost is behind you the garden will make itself known in earnest. There are perennials, herbs – rosemary, thyme, sage, tarragon.

A thought: do you realize that if Joe Orton had lived he'd probably be dead by now? His diaries are in the bookcase by the bed. I found them particularly moving. That desire to create oneself as far from family – mother and father, that is – as possible. And the assholes would say he paid a price for that, but that's not it at all. No.

Don't let the North Africa stuff horrify you. Boys will be boys – especially the English variety.

I guess I think of Orton as as much of an immigrant as you and I are/were. I mean, at least we were brought here at ages young enough so that . . . That's not clear. What I mean to say is that he didn't know the customs of his new world. Christ, I don't know why I'm going orf like this. I should stick to describing paintings and let you do the political analyses. I think I'm afraid you're going to disapprove of him and therefore of me. Simple as that. After all this time. Crazy.

Also – not to change the subject – onions, garlic, asparagus. I dug the ditch for the asparagus myself three years ago. They will be in full power now. Two weeks in June – maybe three.

I remember a drive across the country years ago – the same route you took, I think – recognizing along the side of Highway 80 the flowers of Jerusalem artichoke. Everywhere. In such abundance I doubted my perception, and Jack thought I had become dangerously obsessive. I was like a kid counting Fords to pass the time. Into Iowa, Nebraska, and on and on. Not an artichoke at all, of course. Girasole, turning to the sun. Sister (or brother) to the sunflower. The small yellow heads will bloom in summer – I planted the garden boundary with them.

Being a big brother dies hard. Remember *Night of the Hunter*? Big brother and little sister running, finding Lillian Gish and her rifle – 'I've got something trapped in the barn'. Whatever. My need to look out for you, teach, worry. Even after all the years of separation, and the early rupture we both endured.

The food of the Indians. In the deep freeze of the ground across those thousands of miles; spreading and spreading in spring and summer, then blooming, stretching. Crazy Horse may have roasted their ancestors over a fire on the run. I still love him.

I remember you writing to me a few years ago about the old woman you encountered; you know, the one with the story about the boy she took to Father Flanagan? How she told him about the same thing? You were so angry when you wrote. So she wasn't Lillian Gish with rifle, house filled with castaway children, evil lurking in the barn, wounded, at bay. Who is? At least it wasn't a nuthouse. Boys' Town, I mean.

Anyway, I planted them after I got your letter, the following spring, thinking about the boy. He may have been okay, you know.

(She smiled. Poured a small glass of vodka. Returned to her place at his desk.)

Okay. Back to practical things: if you feel like it, you can have Sam Haines at the service station till the garden for you. He'll refuse money but likes a bottle of Scotch. A nice big man. Very quiet. Almost startlingly ugly; something ate away a good deal of his lower jaw. The Mini-Mart woman says cancer (in a stage whisper), her husband, shrapnel (in a booming voice). Country matters again. But you soon get past his scars. He's the one that told me the lake's haunted. Yes, indeed. Quite a crew supposed to dance among the weeds.

Let's see: movie stars from the time the place was a summer colony; *exclusive*, Sam says. People arrived by private railway car at Northampton and were driven here in a chauffeured Packard, owned (of course) by the local undertaker. Sam's uncle was the driver for a time – for both sets of occasions. It was, still is, a small village, even with the arrival of summer people, and the undertaker had a hard time making ends meet – even during epidemics. Sam explained all this as if excusing the undertaker, his uncle, himself. People here have to make money off outsiders but they don't like it. Well, the undertaker's long gone now, or else I might be tempted to stick around and do one last good deed. 'Die for the nice man, Billy.' Smile.

Back to . . . Sam's a discreet man, shy really, but did say that the cases of booze usually equaled the cases of clothes. And that there was 'talk'. I ask you, where would we be without 'talk'? The usual stuff: loose women, drinking, skinny dips, and one old boy saw – for this Sam dropped his voice – 'an unformed baby peeping out the drain at one end of the lake'. Sam's uncle was called, the undertaker notified, and the little thing was taken care of. After that, no more were found, but the place was finally abandoned when one of the 'stars' died of blood poisoning. Her death, Sam said, was blamed on Christian Science.

The ghosts, by the way, are ladies only.

Who else? Civil War widows. Sam says those are the furious ones. When the waves roll across the lake in summer before a storm, there may be whitecaps. If so – although this seems highly unlikely – but who am I to say? – if so, you will know the widows are especially pissed off. There will be a whiff of salt in the air, because the widows, Sam says, are weeping. And the lake turns for an instant – salt. I suppose the kind of tears you shed when your fury has no place else to go – concentrated, thick.

It seems the place had an inordinate number of men die at Antietam (what would be ordinate?) and the ladies never quite regained their cool.

Finally, there are those known only as the tongueless women. These really are the most interesting, probably for me because they are the ones closest to us: Watchmakers. If you look across the lake from the cottage you will see a slender chimney. That's all that remains of the factory where they worked, except for some bricks scattered around. They were not under some spell or hexed. (Except they were.) No call for ducking stool or scold's bridle. Their tongues fell out, rotted in their heads, Sam says, because of the radium they used to dot above the numbers on the watchfaces. They licked the brushes with their tongues.

Sam says they want to warn people that there's radium in the waters of the lake, but they can't speak. Of course they can't, they have no tongues – and if that weren't enough, the poor dears are dead. You'll know they're there by the shimmer of light on the water – early in the morning – a foolish fire.

Atmosphere, my dear.

It's too much sometimes.

Seed catalogues and seeds from last year (still good) are in the basket on top of the fridge. And you can get sets of tomatoes and peppers and lettuce, etc., from the farm up the road. 'Up' means away from the village. It's run by a woman who takes in teenagers every summer. Sends them back to the city on Labor Day and waits for them to return. And they do, most of them.

Now, look, don't worry about me. You were sweet to

136

offer but it's really better this way. These people know what to do and my mind (or what's left of it) will be at rest. And I still have friends in the city. Yes.

Would that I were going to a villa in Tuscany and we were ten friends telling stories; wonderful, strange, bawdy stories to lift our spirits and pass the time, while the cloud forsakes us.

Speaking of the ladies under the lake, remember that incredible image of the mother in *Night of the Hunter*? Shelley Winters sitting upright in a Model T with her hair mingling with the weeds? Perhaps it's something like that? No.

I'm glad you're in the house. I hope you'll want to stay. It's yours in any case. I want a smooth transition.

More practical matters: I have had the place gone over by a cleaning woman — very thorough. Not to worry.

You have the number where I'll be. I'm sure I gave it to you.

(He hadn't.)

Anyway I'll call when I have the chance and see how you're getting along.

(Will he?)

I hope you love this place as much as I have.

Take care of yourself. And remember what they taught us, or what we learned by trial and error: God bless the child that's got his/her own.

Love, Bill

(She hadn't expected it to stop so suddenly.)

PS. Some old clothes you might want to toss are in the oak bureau. Obviously the Goodwill won't want them. Forgive bitterness.

PPS. The family pall is stored in the crawl space. On to Berlin!

137

IV

She put the letter aside, rubbed her hands along the worn ridges of corduroy, trying to raise his scent.

Out of nowhere came their great-grandmother, speaking of the cholera in her girlhood and how the dead were wrapped and swaddled and rolled outside the door, to be carted away, carried off by a man who actually sang, 'Bring out your dead.' An office, the great-grandmother told them, given him for some trespass or other. 'For no one would choose to handle the plague-dead, you see.'

She did not say if he brought artistry to his street-cry. Was he as thrilling as the 'freshee-fishee' man she remembered when their mother opened a box of frozen fishsticks? As looked-forward-to as the 'icee-icee' man she imitated whenever Good Humor rang the bell outside the apartment house? The great-grandmother did not say.

She only said that to this day, on their island of origin, which neither child could remember, there was a cemetery with dirt so alive it was a crime to enter in.

The great-grandmother was impossible – so they all agreed. Telling Bill to stop blowing his nose in the sheets in the middle of the night, telling Jess that boys would sniff at her 'like dogs' once her periods started. Jess was eleven, Bill thirteen, when the old woman died in a state hospital, sitting in a corner running an imaginary iron over an imaginary suit of clothes.

Jess had resented her sorely. Resented particularly being the girl, that she had the responsibility for the old woman while their parents worked and Bill played after-school games. Resented the old woman as a portent – this is what little girls turn into.

She stirs herself to the larder and finds a package of Carr's water biscuits – carefully crumbling a few in her hand she turns her attention to the cardinal puffed out in the snow.

The cardinal receives the crumbs and pokes at them with his beak. What is he doing here all alone?

Back inside she tries to shake off the chill. Laying more wood on the fire, she puts a kettle on, changes her mind, pours another vodka.

She sets the glass on the desk beside her brother's folded letter.

She reads it again.

She tries to compose a response, but he has given her no forwarding address, and for the moment she allows this to stop her.

Tomorrow, she determines, on her way to buy birdseed she will stop at the PO and get his new address. Surely he must have told them?

V

A child is shut on a glass porch. The panes are painted shut. It is early autumn. Through the glass he can hear the hum and crack of someone's radio broadcasting the World Series. It is a hot Indian summer day.

1959. The Dodgers in LA are about to clinch it. He strains to listen to noises from three thousand miles away. But it's so hard to keep his mind on the game.

1959. Jess is twelve; Bill is fourteen. Jess is at this moment sitting in the back of the family's '51 Nash, head out the window, staring at the running board. Tread almost worn away. Her eyes trace the remaining lines. Her mind is on her brother who is shut on the porch. Should she raise her head and focus her eyes two stories up she might see him. She can't.

Mother and father are in the front seat, in their customary places, as she is in hers. They are in the front seat of the car, looking ahead. To the familiar street, comforting, two-family shingle houses, four-family, six-family apartment houses, streetlamps reaching across the pavement in graceful arcs. Children are pedaling two-wheelers with brakes in the rear wheels. Striped polo shirts zip down the hill. The whole scene could be a postcard, advertisement for a heartbreaking state of well-being – but for one thing.

The father presses the gas pedal and the car moves forward – carefully. Away from the house. Away from her brother.

A boy in a glass booth.

It is just past midday. The sun is magnified in the glass and seems to pinpoint the child on the closed-in porch, his skin reddening. There is no shade. Nowhere to hide from the brightness. Sweat gathers at his temples. On his top lip. He drips. The sweat curls his dark-brown hair. There is no relief in this heat, this light. He draws a breath and feels his throat closing. He gags in the heat and the light. Vomiting orange juice and milk and shredded wheat onto the floor of the porch.

In the front seat of the car is a bound notebook. Black and white marbled cardboard cover, it could have held spelling, geography, the dates of historical events. In the blank space for *subject* is written DIARY–PRIVATE PROPERTY. This notebook is wedged tight between the parents, cotton spine against gray wool upholstery.

The parents say nothing to her, nothing at all. There is silence in the car but for her mother's whimpers.

The parents do not explain why they have brought her along. Why should she expect an explanation?

All that has been directed at her all morning is 'Get in the car! Get in the car!' as if a getaway were at hand and she was jeopardizing their lives by dawdling.

The parents say nothing to her, nor to one another, and the father swings the heavy Nash around an intersection, down a hill, and into the parking lot of the Medical Arts building, brick with Tudor detail.

The sky is a cold blue. Amaranthus trees, prehistoric – as prehistoric as the roaches that congregate under the sink –

what she and her brother call 'A-Tree-Grows-in-Brooklyn-trees' surround the cars – yellow.

She is told to wait.

Her mind is on her brother. The wildness of the morning.

His notebook spread wide open at their father's place. Between the toast and coffee and the eggs over-easy. Is he about to catch hell for doodling Crazy Horse across a geometry lesson?

Nothing that ordinary.

A thin film of yellow – almost hard – is over one sentence where she glances. *I think I am.* Her father catches her looking, she knows to look away.

Her father ignores his son, looks directly at her mother, then back at the page.

'Jesus Christ! Jesus Christ!'

He chants it into silence.

'What?' Jess can't help herself. She is commanded to leave the table. 'You, stay.' Bill must remain.

As she leaves, she glances back at the three. Bill's head is hung. 'And don't I have any rights?' She barely hears him; he speaks the words into the placemat.

Later, when she asked him – much later, when they were all grown-up – when she asked him if she should have stuck up for him that morning, he reminded her she was younger, and a girl, and probably had no idea what it was about, and to forget about it.

But she didn't.

'What in Christ's name do you know about rights?'

The father silenced the son.

In her bed, where she lay staring at the ceiling, Jess heard the noises of tears, whispers. A sudden shout from their mother: 'Goddamit! Stop it! Goddamit! Stop it! Don't you know it's a sickness?'

Then silence.

And then the rustle of parents summoning an expert: calling the minister, informing him the son of a cousin was in trouble, getting a name to call. Apologizing that it is an emergency, a Saturday morning, a beautiful day.

They arrange the visit.

The smell of vomit on the glass-enclosed porch only made things worse for him. He began to sob.

She is not at all certain what has gone on. Only that there is something wrong with her brother, and she wishes that she had never wished him dead because he was a boy, and the logical favorite.

She must have waited in the car for over an hour. Needing to use the bathroom. Afraid to leave and ask the people in the diner across the street. Afraid her parents will return and find the Nash abandoned. Their daughter gone.

'Are you trying to worry us to death?'

He thought briefly about smashing the glass with the heavy brass lamp and driving the shards into his wrists, his neck. He did not think about smashing the glass with the heavy brass lamp and sliding through an opening, dropping to the lawn below like a cat, getting away. Nor about taking the lamp by the base and swinging it faster and faster, spinning with it, laying waste to his mother's Hummels, carefully displayed on bric-a-brac shelves.

Jess watched the parents leave the front of the building. They looked as if in mourning, and she realized they had put on their best clothes, the ones they had worn to the great-grandmother's funeral the year before.

They were strangers in a strange land.

They opened the door of the Nash and slid into their places, the mother clasping the notebook to her. With a sigh the father started the car.

'Did you see the doctor?' Jess asked.

'Yes, dear,' her mother responded.

'Is Bill going to be okay?'

'In time.'

The landmarks of the neighborhood went by again: candy store, luncheonette, branch library, the Store of a Million Items, statue to the war dead, bar with pictures of Miss Rheingold contestants in the window, church, and then, almost home, the houses.

VI

Bill took his treatment one afternoon a week, heading at the last bell in one direction while his classmates went their own ways.

Sitting in the office of Dr Blanke, in the Medical Arts, Bill focused his attention as best he could on the figurine on the table beside him. His mind, in this waiting room, could not hold on to words printed on a page. His schoolbooks remained in his schoolbag, resting against the leg of the green leatherette chair in which he sat. The magazines arranged on the low table in front of him went untouched.

Each time he sat there, the fluorescent light flickering overhead, he began by staring at the three-dimensional portrait beside him; an old man with a spindly beard and straw hat, someone's idea of a Chinese fisherman. His bare porcelain feet were drawn up under him on a porcelain rock. He dangled his thin line from his rod, a sliver of bamboo.

Bill thought the old man was one of a kind, like himself, and would probably have been startled to be faced with a line of identical old men on a shelf in the Store of a Million Items. A crate of old men unloaded onto the docks at the foot of the hill from the Medical Arts, all the way from Taiwan, excelsior clinging to their feet.

Bill had not even spoken to the other boy about it, just noted in the diary, *I think I may be. I think I am.* Following those speculations with the only word he had ever heard to describe it.

At the end of the old man's line hung a fish, from a small hook, a fish made of a deep green glass, with tiny bubbles inside. Bill stared at the figurine, then put his head back, curved his spine into a question mark and shut his eyes. He imagined the old man in a safe place, ten thousand miles away, at the edge of a river, clean and cold, in which there were smooth, flat rocks. A thick fog settled around his shoulders, embracing him.

Behind him, on the bank, was a fire which warmed him, over which he would cook his fish.

You could detach the fish from the line. Each time, as the nurse was about to summon him, Bill pocketed the fish, feeling its smooth glassiness, hard and cool, his fist tightening around his amulet, the thing between himself and *cure*, as they fixed the electrodes to his head.

The green fish. Burning. Jelly sandwiches on white bread. A bruise over his left eye where he convulsed against a radiator.

The treatments were expensive. The family left their apartment in the six-family house and moved into a smaller place over a drugstore, underneath a man and a woman who battled almost every night.

The treatments were expensive, and they did not take. He was sent to a tough place up the Hudson, where they taught him carpentry. And when he returned, he knew enough to build some shelves for his mother's spices, and to ask a girl to the Junior Prom.

VII

Jess has read the letter yet again. She is not ready to compose an answer. She folds the letter and puts it between the pages of her ill-kept journal. Ill-kept by moonlight, proud Titania – silly joke.

She begins to arrange her things on top of her brother's desk but cannot make a dent in his presence – nor does she want to.

She sits at the desk for some time.

Bill's green glass fish, which he's had since God knows when, is sitting on a bookshelf. The fish reflects the red of the firelight. Hiroshima fish, she thinks, all of a sudden. And just as suddenly can hear her brother's voice: 'Jesus Christ! Do you have to find images of oppression everywhere?'

Later, in the bath, she slides down against the porcelain. As she lowers her body, the water comes up to her breasts, and two dark knobs poke above the surface of the water like buoys. The water rises to her neck as she lowers herself further.

She has tried her entire life, or so it seems to her, not to see that Indian summer morning as the beginning of the end. The moment when she measured her parents for terror, and saw them as two frightened strangers. She has tried not to blame her brother for this terrible revelation which made her feel unsafe, alone. And the aftermath of that morning only confirmed this, so that when the family finally exploded, she was left only numb.

They had gone on pretending for years. Taking two-week vacations in the tiny summer cottage by the lake, even though finances were stretched to the limit. Without Bill at first, then with him, and she could see them measuring him all the while, and her as well.

There is a window next to the tub and she can see the moonlight skating across the ice. No ghosts yet. Except family.

Their great-grandmother believed in ghosts. Had seen them, she said, 'as clear as day'. Her cinnamon eyes would light at the memory of a handsome sea captain she had encountered in the upstairs gallery of a country house where she had gone for a dance. 'And when I told my host and hostess,' she paused, 'they told me he had been dead for many years.'

Like most children, Jess and Bill had loved the idea of ghosts and begged for more. And the great-grandmother was at her best in the telling.

The water is getting cool. She rises, dripping.

Dry now, clean and robed and warmed, she sits in front of the desk again.

She tacks postcards to the white wall above the desk: Billie Holiday; Chief's robe from the Third Phase; The Second Bible Quilt of Harriet Powers; ANC women.

See, Bill – also the resisters – and the artists. People like you. How long it has taken for her to say that.

Above her postcards Bill had hung the *Magic Glasses* of Edwin Romanzo Elmer. Crystal sugar bowl on a marble counter. Into the crystal is placed the magic – the magnifier, prism, divider of light. The magnifying glass has split the landscape which comes into the scene through a window. On either side is reflected a farmyard, woodpile. The concern for sustenance – marble surface for kneading bread, sugar bowl, woodpile – warmth, future. In the center of the magnifying glass – where the light has been split – is a sliver of dark.

VIII

She had seen no ghosts, took the foolish fire over the lake for what it was.

But the spring was as Bill had promised. On a walk one morning in the woods around the lake she found the first (at least, the first to her) ladyslippers. Dewdrops clung to them. They seemed to have sprung out of the dry needles of the forest floor.

She found herself at the end of the lake, near to the slender chimney Bill had written about. Bricks scattered on the ground, the consistency of stale cake, crumbly. She picked up a brick and could trace the cracks in it, the pieces of sand, clay, whatever came together to make it into something which would support a building, become a building. Poking her foot through the needles revealed something shiny. The delicate wand of a sweep second hand.

IX

May 31, 1988

Dear Bill,
Today they had a celebration on the common for Memorial Day – you probably remember.

Nothing like beginning a letter with a *memento mori* – sorry.

I drove by as it was going on and saw men in uniform, fatigues, women in hats and summer dresses and white gloves, a few children and a few old men. The minister presiding over all. Then a roll-call by a woman wearing a Gold Star. Everyone gathered around the statue to the Union dead, the drummer boy. The scratch of the 'Battle Hymn of the Republic' in the air, broadcast over a loudspeaker set on the porch of the church. And then some lanky boy in blue jeans and white T-shirt – straight out of *Seventeenth Summer* – blew Taps. And after that people drifted away.

The whole thing moved me, appealed to the historian in me. Later, Sam Haines came by the house (he asked to be remembered to you) and offered to rototill the garden. He told me it was a little late but figured I was too shy to ask, or maybe didn't know to ask. He said it was the usual arrangement that he could keep any pieces of glass or china or metal he might find during the tilling. Said he used the stuff 'for decoration'. I said sure. You only mentioned a bottle of Scotch to me and I'll get that in the morning. Maybe he never told you about the other? Well, it's no big deal. Interesting though.

His face is at first startling, as you say, but there's something so calming about his presence.

I am sitting here at your desk, writing this, watching the lake, but no whitecaps yet. I would have thought Memorial Day, the remnant of Taps carrying across the water, would have stirred your widows?

Overheard at the Mini-Mart:

First woman: I hope the Democrats get in in November and do something about this homeless problem. I'm tired of tripping over people when I go up to Boston. All the Republicans know to spend money on is guns.

Second woman: Do you want to be invaded by the Russians?

First woman: At least we'd have free housing.

Second woman: Yes, but what kind of housing? Twenty people in one room.

Oh dear.

I'll also go up the road tomorrow and get some sets. Tomatoes mostly, lettuce, broccoli. Sam asked me what I intended to plant and then advised me about bugs. Cutting a collar for the broccoli out of aluminium foil to deceive the cutworms – one piece of advice. Here again I'm telling you something you already know.

The place just gets more beautiful. The asparagus is coming along. Would it be worth it to you to have me send some down by bus or something? Let me know. Or do you just want it here – that's what I figured, but thought I'd ask anyway. It's a spectacular green right now and the spears are beginning to poke through the earth. The Jerusalem artichoke is on its/their way too.

You know, it's funny. What's funny is that you still see me as this hothead — as hotheaded as the little girl in the schoolyard (one of the 'not-born-heres' as the principal called us) who smashed a girl's glasses when she made another girl cry. 'I am in the world to change the world,' the grown-up version of that little girl told you once, and you called the words (and me too?) 'impossibly dangerous'. Why didn't I, that morning, do something? If I could fight for a stranger why couldn't I fight for you? Because they were our parents? Because the whole scene was so crazy, the threat of calamity so pervasive? Ma always said I cared more for strangers than for family, remember? A place was cleared in me that morning twenty-five years ago. I was emptied. I never saw any one of us the same way again.

For years I blamed you of course. Thinking that I had to be the good girl *par excellence* to make up for you, the bad boy who left the task to me. Thinking, 'Why couldn't he just take his medicine?' You went off without a word and at night, night after bloody night, I would hear Ma crying as Pa slipped deeper and deeper into his silences. Two terrified people.

She looks up from the letter; across the water are two figures, strolling arm in arm, out of a tintype. No. Probably just a couple of aging hippies, never having outgrown their granny dresses, still seeing the world through their granny glasses.

I thought for a moment I saw your ghosts.

Oh, shit. She tears the page across and begins the letter again.

Keeper of All Souls

November 2nd was the day Sam made.

Just after the hullabaloo of Halloween, as hand-carved pumpkins shriveled on folks' porches and stoops, the parade of weekend leaf-peepers diminished, and fall began to bump against winter, Sam's day came and went.

The air was crisp, the church glistened white on the common, fallen leaves crunched underfoot, the sky reflected in the cold waters of the lake.

A postcard, yes, but it did look like that.

A rack of postcards spun inside the door of SAM'S SERVICE STATION, as the sign in front read. Spun slowly, urged on by the hot-air vent in the floor below. Fall and winter scenes mostly, since Mrs Sam re-arranged the rack every few months. Mostly scenes shot during the forties and fifties or so, but a stranger would never know, since there were neither cars nor people in the pictures to give the time away. Timeless — but only to the eye ignorant of the history of the village, someone passing through in haste, eager to get somewhere else. In one shot, elms stood bare against a blue sky, when elms encircled the common before the Dutch Elm struck. In another, the watch factory was intact, had smoke streaming from its chimney, and a legend reading: FINEST TIMEPIECES IN NEW ENGLAND MANUFACTURED HERE.

Sam's was an old-fashioned gas station; no fancy pumps, one greasepit, outdoor thermometer advertising *Royal Crown Cola*, a ladies' room with chintz curtains and a calendar from the local undertaker — put there by Mrs Sam, 'to make women think'.

Sam had switched petroleum companies several times over

the years. On the disk atop the pole in front of the station you could detect the shadow of a star underneath the faint outline of a flying horse which rested on a delicate scallop shell. These pentimenti reminded Sam of times past and he would not neaten the sign, not even when the new dealer offered to replace the entire thing, pole and all, with the logo of the latest corporate giant – huge and ugly letters, no image at all.

Mrs Sam had charge of the ladies' room, and Sam took charge of the men's. On the wall above the single urinal and over the rusted sink, bright painted letters spoke:
IDLENESS IS THE SEPULCHRE OF THE LIVING MAN
KEEP NO MORE CATS THAN WILL KILL MICE
THERE IS AN ALL-SEEING EYE WATCHING YOU

Once one man emerged, hands dripping, eyes lit, asking Sam, 'Did you write those words?'

'Which ones?'

'The ones about the all-seeing eye.'

Sam nodded.

'I'm a Christian too,' the man spoke too enthusiastically, 'read this.' He thrust something printed into Sam's hands.

Sam acknowledged the man's offering with another nod, then let the booklet slide to the floor.

'A man's beliefs are his most intimate thing,' he spoke aloud, softly, then went out back for his brush and paint, adding that thought to the wall.

Out back, behind the station, was another, much smaller building where Sam kept his paints and other things. This had a sign over the door also: SAM'S WORKSHOP. KEEP OUT. And people did. Even his wife.

This was Sam's place of retreat and meditation, where he got his ideas and planned things. Here, he said, he became 'plain'.

Against one wall he had fashioned an altar from aluminium foil over wood. The altar rose from floor to ceiling, and stretched from side to side of the small room. On its front shelf were things Sam arranged and re-arranged, as his vision moved him. Things collected. Things the earth had yielded after a summer downpour, the spring thaw. Things the blades of his tiller turned up. Shards working their way back to the surface. Sam walked through the village, pushing his tiller with one hand, a canvas sack in the other, eyes downcast. You never know what you might find.

Pieces of colored glass, fragments of medicine bottles, Sunday china, everyday ware. A piece of brick. Rusted watchface. Glass-headed, cloth-bodied dolly. Spent shells. Rubber nipples. Ribbon. Wooden letters from a printer's tray. Ring of skeleton keys.

Every place on the altar is cluttered with relics. Everything man-made.

A small clothbound book with *Record* scrolled across the cover is at one end of the shelf. This is 'Sam's Book of the Dead', as is written on the first page, in which he enters the names of the dead on the day of All Souls.

That done, he sits back and sings the dead to sleep. He thought it was the least he could do.

MICHELLE CLIFF

No Telephone to Heaven

'One of the finest and most moving novels of the past year.

'In this tale of identity and nation-hood Cliff evokes a Jamaica full of contradiction and complexity, a country where history and politics are played out in surroundings of overwhelming physical beauty. Slowly the Jamaican diaspora is revealed through the novel's main character, Clare Savage, whose family emigrates to the US when she is twelve . . .

'Clare's emotional and physical journey back to Jamaica and a positive identification of herself as Jamaican takes the form of a fascinating voyage through the polarities and dualities of race and sexuality, the relationships between the first and third worlds and slavery and modern patterns of emigration. Cliff powerfully evokes the historical myths and truths of Jamaican and Black Americans, and the beauty and anguish of modern Jamaica.' *City Limits*

'Michelle Cliff is a remarkable author' *Guardian*

'Vividly and passionately written' *Financial Times*

'Potent and very moving' *Sunday Times*

'Full of razors and blossoms and clarity'
Toni Morrison

'A novel of great beauty' *Marxism Today*

AGOTA KRISTOF

The Notebook

'With war raging, some time in the future or the past, a woman takes her twin sons far away to stay in a forest with her mother, known locally as The Witch. Kristof's nightmarish tale is about the twins' search for the means of survival in an alien adult world . . . Her two protagonists lose themselves in a world of games and secret codes, removing themselves to a subterranean world of the imagination beyond the reach of their elders. Around them, the world is falling to battle, bestiality and abject cruelty. Kristof seems to be writing on the edge of anxiety, surrounded by terror and pleasure. The reader swings by his heels until the book rushes to his head. It's that good. A triumphant debut. Roll on the sequel' *Blitz*

'Closing this chillingly unsentimental first novel, I felt that the author had contrived to say absolutely *everything* about the Second World War and its aftermath in Central Europe . . . With a trio of quite terrifying sentences, the narrative actually ends in the most haunting and unexpected manner imaginable'
Sunday Times

'A parable for our troubled century . . . just, harsh, strangely moving' *Observer*

MICHÈLE ROBERTS

The Wild Girl

In the parched soil of Provence, a fifth gospel has been discovered, Mary Magdalene's account of Jesus' teaching and her relationship with him. It is a book of revelation, for it unveils a new Christianity, one which embraces the female equally with the male and acknowledges and celebrates women's spirituality. It is also a passionate story of love and search, of separation and rebirth, centred on Mary as the wellspring of womanhood.

The Wild Girl offers a brilliant and moving vision that is also startlingly modern in its conclusions. It confirms Michèle Roberts' stature as one of Britain's most talented and exciting writers.

'An assured tour de force of passion . . . the power with which it reclaims spiritual and sexual strength for women cannot be ignored' *Time Out*

'Bold and moving' *Guardian*

'Michèle Roberts is intelligent and passionate; by her rich use of symbols and metaphors she transforms feminist cliché into something alive and moving' *TLS*

JEANETTE WINTERSON

Boating for Beginners

'Winterson has re-written The Book of Genesis and
turned it into a surreal Cecil B De Mille epic. Feminism
and Twentieth Century kitchenware run riot in the
ancient city of Ur; Noah is Howard Hughes crossed
with Frankenstein — an eccentric overseer of thriving
capitalism who makes "God" "by accident out of a
piece of gâteau and a giant electric toaster."

'The result is a tetchy, omnipotent icecream cone who
decides to drown all the decadence of Winterson's
world (and, curiously, that world resembles
Queensway) in a flood — out of which, of course, a
more fitting myth can be born, ie that God is a
benevolent old man with a white beard who loves us all.

'Occasionally, Winterson ceases to be a jester and
seriously explores the power of myth ("they explain the
universe while allowing the universe to go on being
unexplained . . .") and of faith ("when the heart revolts
it wants outrageous things that cannot possibly be
factual . . ."). I could have done with a bit more of this
and less jokes about fast food. But then I prefer
depressing books, and Winterson has proved with
Oranges Are Not The Only Fruit how popular her wit
is' Jane Solanas, *Time Out*

'If you find the Monty Python *Life of Brian* amusing,
this is your comic book of revelations'
Andrew Sinclair, *The Times*

A Selected List of Titles Available from Minerva

While every effort is made to keep prices low, it is sometimes necessary to increase prices at short notice. Mandarin Paperbacks reserves the right to show new retail prices on covers which may differ from those previously advertised in the text or elsewhere.

The prices shown below were correct at the time of going to press.

Fiction

☐	7493 9026 3	**I Pass Like Night**	Jonathan Ames	£3.99	BX
☐	7493 9006 9	**The Tidewater Tales**	John Bath	£4.99	BX
☐	7493 9004 2	**A Casual Brutality**	Neil Blessondath	£4.50	BX
☐	7493 9028 2	**Interior**	Justin Cartwright	£3.99	BC
☐	7493 9002 6	**No Telephone to Heaven**	Michelle Cliff	£3.99	BX
☐	7493 9028 X	**Not Not While the Giro**	James Kelman	£4.50	BX
☐	7493 9011 5	**Parable of the Blind**	Gert Hofmann	£3.99	BC
☐	7493 9010 7	**The Inventor**	Jakov Lind	£3.99	BC
☐	7493 9003 4	**Fall of the Imam**	Nawal El Saadewi	£3.99	BC

Non-Fiction

☐	7493 9012 3	**Days in the Life**	Jonathon Green	£4.99	BC
☐	7493 9019 0	**In Search of J D Salinger**	Ian Hamilton	£4.99	BX
☐	7493 9023 9	**Stealing from a Deep Place**	Brian Hall	£3.99	BX
☐	7493 9005 0	**The Orton Diaries**	John Lahr	£5.99	BC
☐	7493 9014 X	**Nora**	Brenda Maddox	£6.99	BC

All these books are available at your bookshop or newsagent, or can be ordered direct from the publisher. Just tick the titles you want and fill in the form below. Available in:
BX: British Commonwealth excluding Canada
BC: British Commonwealth including Canada

Mandarin Paperbacks, Cash Sales Department, PO Box 11, Falmouth, Cornwall TR10 9EN.

Please send cheque or postal order, no currency, for purchase price quoted and allow the following for postage and packing:

UK   80p for the first book, 20p for each additional book ordered to a maximum charge of £2.00.

BFPO   80p for the first book, 20p for each additional book.

Overseas   £1.50 for the first book, £1.00 for the second and 30p for each additional book
including Eire   thereafter.

NAME (Block letters) ....

ADDRESS ....

....

....